*...ution*

Eileen Chang (1920–95) was born into an aristocratic family in Shanghai. Her father, deeply traditional in his ways, was an opium addict; her mother, partly educated in England, was a sophisticated woman of cosmopolitan tastes. Their unhappy marriage ended in divorce, and Chang eventually ran away from her father – who had beaten her for defying her stepmother, then locked her in her room for nearly half a year. Chang studied literature at the University of Hong Kong, but the Japanese attack on the city in 1941 forced her to return to occupied Shanghai, where she was able to publish the stories and essays that soon made her a literary star. In 1944 Chang married Hu Lancheng, a Japanese sympathizer whose sexual infidelities led to their divorce three years later. The rise of the communist influence made it increasingly difficult for Chang to continue living in Shanghai; she moved to Hong Kong in 1952, then emigrated to the United States three years later. She remarried and held various posts as writer in residence; in 1969 she obtained a more permanent position as a researcher at Berkeley. Two novels both commissioned in the 1950s by the United States information service as anti-communist propaganda, *The Rice Sprout Song* and *Naked Earth*, were followed by a third, *The Rouge of the North* (1967), which expanded on her early novella, 'The Golden Cangue'. Chang continued writing essays and stories in Chinese, scripts for Hong Kong films, and began work on an English translation of the famous Qing novel *The Sing-Song Girls of Shanghai*. In spite of the tremendous revival of interest in her work that began in Taiwan and Hong Kong in the 1970s and which later spread to mainland China, Chang became ever more reclusive as she grew older. Eileen Chang was found dead in her Los Angeles apartment in September 1995. Her novel *Eighteen Springs*, never before translated into English, is forthcoming in Penguin Modern Classics.

Julia Lovell is a lecturer in Chinese history at the University of London. She is the author of *The Great Wall: China Against the World, 1000 BC – AD 2000*, and *The Politics of Cultural Capital: China's Quest for a Nobel Prize in Literature*. She has translated the novels *Serve the People* by Yan Lianke and *A Dict*... collection of novellas by Zhu W... *a*.

D1347499

Karen S. Kingsbury has lived in Chinese-speaking cities for nearly two decades. She taught English in Chonqing on the Whitman-in-China programme, studied Chinese in Taipei and, for fourteen years, taught English Language and Literature at Tunghai University in Taichung. Her Columbia doctoral dissertation was on Eileen Chang, and she has published previous translations of Chang's essays and fiction in *Renditions* and in *The Columbia Anthology of Modern Chinese Literature*. She lives in Seattle.

Janet Ng teaches at the City University of New York, College of Staten Island. Her works include *The Experience of Modernity: Chinese Autobiography of the Early Twentieth Century* (2003) and *May Fourth Women Writers: Memoirs* (1996).

Janice Wickeri is a freelance translator and editor. She has an MFA from San Francisco State University, edits the *Chinese Theological Review* and was formerly managing editor of *Renditions*.

Simon Patton is a freelance literary translator. He teaches Chinese and translation part-time at the University of Queensland, Australia, and co-edits the China domain of Poetry International Web (china.poetry internationalweb.org).

Eva Hung was born in Hong Kong and received her PhD from London University. She served for twenty years as editor of *Renditions* and is well known for her work in literary translation as well as Chinese translation history.

# EILEEN CHANG

# *Lust, Caution*
# *and Other Stories*

*Translated by Julia Lovell, Karen S. Kingsbury, Janet Ng*
*(with Janice Wickeri), Simon Patton and Eva Hung*

*Edited and with an Afterword by Julia Lovell*

PENGUIN BOOKS

PENGUIN CLASSICS

Published by the Penguin Group
Penguin Books Ltd, 80 Strand, London WC2R ORL, England
Penguin Group (USA) Inc., 375 Hudson Street, New York, New York 10014, USA
Penguin Group (Canada), 90 Eglinton Avenue East, Suite 700, Toronto, Ontario, Canada M4P 2Y3
(a division of Pearson Penguin Canada Inc.)
Penguin Ireland, 25 St Stephen's Green, Dublin 2, Ireland (a division of Penguin Books Ltd)
Penguin Group (Australia), 250 Camberwell Road, Camberwell, Victoria 3124, Australia
(a division of Pearson Australia Group Pty Ltd)
Penguin Books India Pvt Ltd, 11 Community Centre, Panchsheel Park, New Delhi – 110 017, India
Penguin Group (NZ), 67 Apollo Drive, Rosedale, North Shore 0632, New Zealand
(a division of Pearson New Zealand Ltd)
Penguin Books (South Africa) (Pty) Ltd, 24 Sturdee Avenue, Rosebank, Johannesburg 2196, South Africa

Penguin Books Ltd, Registered Offices: 80 Strand, London WC2R ORL, England

www.penguin.com

This collection first published in Penguin Classics 2007
1

Stories copyright © by the Estate of Eileen Chang, 1944, 1945, 1947, 1979
Translation of 'Lust, Caution' copyright © Julia Lovell, 2007
Translation of 'In the Waiting Room' copyright © Karen S. Kingsbury, 2007
Translations of 'Great Felicity' and 'Traces of Love' first published in *Renditions*, No. 45 (Spring 1996),
reprinted in *Traces of Love and Other Stories* by Eileen Chang (ed. Eva Hung) in Renditions Paperbacks,
published by the Research Centre for Translation, The Chinese University of Hong Kong, copyright
© The Chinese University of Hong Kong, 2000
Translation of 'Steamed Osmanthus Flower: Ah Xiao's Unhappy Autumn' first published in *Traces of Love
and Other Stories* by Eileen Chang (ed. Eva Hung) in Renditions Paperbacks, published by the Research
Centre for Translation, The Chinese University of Hong Kong, copyright © The Chinese University of
Hong Kong, 2000. Reprinted by permission of the Research Centre for Translation, The Chinese University
of Hong Kong.
Editor's Afterword and A Guide to Pronunciation copyright © Julia Lovell, 2007
All rights reserved

The moral right of the translators and editor has been asserted

Set in 11.25/14 pt PostScript Monotype Dante
Typeset by Rowland Phototypesetting Ltd, Bury St Edmunds, Suffolk
Printed in England by Clays Ltd, St Ives plc

Except in the United States of America, this book is sold subject
to the condition that it shall not, by way of trade or otherwise, be lent,
re-sold, hired out, or otherwise circulated without the publisher's
prior consent in any form of binding or cover other than that in
which it is published and without a similar condition including this
condition being imposed on the subsequent purchaser

ISBN: 978-0-141-03438-6

# Contents

| LONDON BOROUGH OF WANDSWORTH | |
|---|---|
| 501298158 | |
| **Askews** | 03-Jan-2008 |
| AF  ZHAN | £7.99 |
| | WWX0002527/0055 |

# LUST, CAUTION

Though it was still daylight, the hot lamp was shining full-beam over the mahjong table. Diamond rings flashed under its glare as their wearers clacked and reshuffled their tiles. The table-cloth, tied down over the table legs, stretched out into a sleek plain of blinding white. The harsh artificial light silhouetted to full advantage the generous curve of Jiazhi's bosom, and laid bare the elegant lines of her hexagonal face, its beauty somehow accentuated by the imperfectly narrow forehead, by the careless, framing wisps of hair. Her makeup was understated, except for the glossily rouged arcs of her lips. Her hair she had pinned nonchalantly back from her face, then allowed to hang down to her shoulders. Her sleeveless cheongsam of electric blue moiré satin reached to the knees, its shallow, rounded collar standing only half an inch tall, in the Western style. A brooch fixed to the collar matched her diamond-studded sapphire button earrings.

The two ladies – *taitais* – immediately to her left and right were both wearing black wool capes, each held fast at the neck by a heavy double gold chain that snaked out from beneath the cloak's turned-down collar. Isolated from the rest of the world by Japanese occupation, Shanghai had elaborated a few native fashions. Thanks to the extravagantly inflated price of gold in the occupied territories, gold chains as thick as these were now fabulously expensive. But somehow, functionally worn in place of a collar button, they managed to avoid the taint of vulgar ostentation, thereby offering their owners the perfect pretext for parading their wealth on excursions about the city. For these excellent reasons, the cape and gold chain had become the favoured uniform of the wives of officials serving in Wang Jingwei's puppet government. Or perhaps they were following the lead of Chongqing, the Chinese Nationalist regime's wartime capital, where black cloaks were very much in vogue among the elegant ladies of the political glitterati.

Yi Taitai was *chez elle*, so she had dispensed with her own cape; but even without it, her figure still seemed to bell outward from her neck, with all the weight the years had put on her. She'd met Jiazhi two years earlier in Hong Kong, after she and her husband had left Chongqing – and the Nationalist government – together with Wang Jingwei. Not long before the couple took refuge on the island, one of Wang Jingwei's lieutenants, Zeng Zhongming, had been assassinated in Hanoi, and so Wang's followers in Hong Kong were keeping their heads down. Yi Taitai, nonetheless, was determined to go shopping. During the war, goods were scarce in both the unconquered interior and the occupied territories of the Mainland; Yi Taitai had no intention of wasting the golden purchasing opportunity offered by a stopover in the commercial paradise of Hong Kong. Someone in her circle introduced her to Jiazhi – the beautiful young wife of Mr Mai, a local businessman – who chaperoned her on her shopping trips. If you wanted to navigate Hong Kong's emporiums, you had to have a local along: you were expected to haggle over prices even in the biggest department stores, and if you couldn't speak Cantonese, all the traders would overcharge you wickedly. Mr Mai was in import–export and, like all business people, delighted in making political friends. So of course the couple were incessantly hospitable to Yi Taitai, who was in turn extremely grateful. After the bombing of Pearl Harbor and the fall of Hong Kong, Mr Mai went out of business. To make some extra money for the family, Mai Taitai decided to do a little smuggling herself, and travelled to Shanghai with a few luxury goods – watches, Western medicines, perfumes, stockings – to sell. Yi Taitai very naturally invited her to stay with them.

'We went to Shuyu, that Szechuanese restaurant, yesterday,' Yi Taitai was telling the first black cape. 'Mai Taitai hadn't been.'

'Oh, really?'

'We haven't seen you here for a few days, Ma Taitai.'

'I've been busy – a family matter,' Ma Taitai mumbled amid the twittering of the mahjong tiles.

Yi Taitai's lips thinned into a smile. 'She went into hiding because it was her turn to buy dinner.'

Jiazhi suspected that Ma Taitai was jealous. Ever since Jiazhi had arrived, she had been the centre of attention.

'Liao Taitai took us all out last night. She's been on such a winning streak the last couple of days,' Yi Taitai went on to Ma Taitai. 'At the restaurant, I bumped into that young Mr Li and his wife and invited them to join us. When he said they were waiting for guests of their own, I told him they should all join us. After all, it isn't often that Liao Taitai gives dinner parties. Then it turned out Mr Li had invited so many guests we couldn't fit them all around our table. Even with extra chairs we couldn't all squeeze in, so Liao Taitai had to sit behind me like a sing-song girl at a banquet. "What a beauty I've picked for myself tonight," I joked. "I'm too old a piece of tofu for you to swallow," she replied. "Old tofu tastes the spiciest," I told her! Oh, how we laughed. She laughed so much her pockmarks turned red.'

More laughter around the mahjong table.

While Yi Taitai was still updating Ma Taitai on the goings-on of the past couple of days, Mr Yi came in, dressed in a grey suit, and nodded at his three female guests.

'You started early today.'

He stood behind his wife, watching the game. The wall behind him was swathed in heavy, yellowish-brown wool curtains printed with a brick-red phoenix-tail fern design, each blade almost six feet long. Zhou Fohai, Wang Jingwei's second-in-command, had a pair; and so, therefore, did they. False French windows, and enormous drapes to cover them, were all the rage just then. Because of the war, fabrics were in short supply; floor-length curtains such as those hanging behind Mr Yi – using up an entire bolt of cloth, with extra wastage from pattern matching – were a conspicuous extravagance. Standing against the huge ferns of his backdrop, Yi looked even shorter than usual. His face was pale, finely drawn, and crowned by a receding hairline that faded away into petal-shaped peaks above his temples. His nose was distinguished by its narrowed, almost rat-like tip.

'Is that ring of yours three carats, Ma Taitai?' Yi Taitai asked. 'The day before yesterday, Pin Fen brought a five-carat diamond to show me, but it didn't sparkle like yours.'

'I've heard Pin Fen's things are better than the stuff in the shops.'

'It is convenient to have things brought to your home, I suppose. And you can hold on to them for a few days, while you decide. And sometimes she has things you can't get elsewhere. Last time, she showed me a yellow kerosene diamond, but *he* wouldn't buy it.' She glanced icily at Mr Yi before going on: 'How much do you imagine something like that would cost now? A perfect kerosene diamond: a dozen ounces of gold per carat? Two? Three? Pin Fen says no one's selling kerosene or pink diamonds at the moment, for any price. Everyone's hoarding them, waiting for the price to get even more insane.'

'Didn't you feel how heavy it was?' Mr Yi laughed. 'Ten carats. You wouldn't have been able to play mahjong with that rock on your finger.'

The edges of the table glittered like a diamond exhibition, Jiazhi thought, every pair of hands glinting ostentatiously – except hers. She should have left her jadeite ring back in its box, she realized; to spare herself all those sneering glances.

'Stop making fun of me!' Yi Taitai sulked as she moved out one of her counters. The black cape opposite Ma Taitai clatteringly opened out her winning hand, and a sudden commotion of laughter and lament broke the thread of conversation.

As the gamblers busily set to calculating their wins and losses, Mr Yi motioned slightly at Jiazhi with his chin towards the door.

She immediately glanced at the two black capes on either side of her. Fortunately, neither seemed to have noticed. She paid out the chips she had lost, took a sip from her teacup, then suddenly exclaimed: 'That memory of mine! I have a business appointment at three o'clock, I'd forgotten all about it. Mr Yi, will you take my place until I get back?'

'I won't allow it!' Yi Taitai protested. 'You can't just run away like that without warning us in advance.'

'And just when I thought my luck was changing,' muttered the winning black cape.

'I suppose we could ask Liao Taitai to come over. Go and telephone her,' Yi Taitai went on to Jiazhi. 'At least stay until she gets here.'

'I really need to go now.' Jiazhi looked at her watch. 'I'm

going to be late – I arranged to have coffee with a broker. Mr Yi can take my place.'

'I'm busy this afternoon,' Mr Yi excused himself. 'Tomorrow I'll play all night.'

'That Wang Jiazhi!' Yi Taitai liked referring to Jiazhi by her full maiden name, as if they had known each other since they were girls. 'I'll make you pay for this – you're going to treat us all to dinner tonight!'

'You can't let your guest buy you dinner,' Ma Taitai objected.

'I'm siding with Yi Taitai,' the other black cape put in.

They needed to tread carefully around their hostess on the subject of her young house guest. Although Yi Taitai was easily old enough to be Jiazhi's mother, there had never been any talk of formalizing their relationship, of adopting her as a goddaughter. Yi Taitai was a little unpredictable, at the age she was now. Although she had a dowager's fondness for keeping young, pretty women clustered around her – like a galaxy of stars reflecting glory on to the moon around which they circulated – she was not yet too old for flashes of feminine jealousy.

'All right, all right,' Jiazhi said. 'I'll take you all out to dinner tonight. But you won't be in the party, Mr Yi, if you don't take my place now.'

'Do, Mr Yi! Mahjong's no fun with only three. Play just for a little, while Ma Taitai telephones for a replacement.'

'I really do have a prior engagement.' Whenever Mr Yi spoke of official business, his voice sank to an almost inaudibly discreet mutter. 'Someone else will come along soon.'

'We all know how busy Mr Yi is,' Ma Taitai said.

Was she insinuating something, Jiazhi wondered, or were nerves getting the better of her? Observing him smile and banter, Jiazhi even began to read a flattering undertone into Ma

Taitai's remark, as if she knew that he wanted other people to coax the details of his conquest out of him. Perhaps success, she speculated, can turn the heads of even the professionally secretive.

It was getting far too dangerous. If the job wasn't done today, if the thing were to drag on any longer, Yi Taitai would surely find them out.

He walked off while she was still exhaustingly negotiating her exit with his wife. After finally extricating herself, she returned briefly to her room. As she finished hurriedly tidying her hair and makeup – there was too little time to change her clothes – the maidservant arrived to tell her the car was waiting for her at the door. Getting in, she gave the chauffeur instructions to drive her to a café; once arrived, she sent him back home.

As it was only mid-afternoon, the café was almost deserted. Its large interior was lit by wall lamps with pleated apricot silk shades, its floor populated by small round tables covered in cloths of fine white linen jacquard – an old-fashioned, middle-brow kind of establishment. She made a call from the public telephone on the counter. After four rings, she hung up and redialled, muttering 'wrong number' to herself, for fear the cashier might think her behaviour strange.

That was the code. The second time, someone answered.

'Hello?'

Thank goodness – it was Kuang Yumin. Even now, she was terrified she might have to speak to Liang Runsheng, though he was usually very careful to let others get to the phone first.

'It's me,' she replied in Cantonese. 'Everyone well?'

'All fine. How about yourself?'

'I'll be going shopping this afternoon, but I'm not sure when.'

'No problem. We'll wait for you. Where are you now?'

'Xiafei Road.'

'Fine.'

A pause.

'Nothing else then?' Her hands felt cold, but she was somehow warmed by the sound of a familiar voice.

'No, nothing.'

'I might go right now.'

'We'll be there, don't worry. See you later.'

She hung up and exited to hail a pedicab.

If they didn't finish it off today, she couldn't stay on at the Yis' – not with all those great bejewelled cats watching her every move. Maybe she should have found an excuse to move out as soon as she had hooked him. He could have found her a place somewhere: the last couple of times they'd met in apartments, different ones each time, left vacant by British or Americans departed to war camps. But that probably would have made everything even more complicated – how would she have known what time he was coming? He might have suddenly descended upon her at any moment. Or if they had fixed a time in advance, urgent business might have forced him to cancel at the last minute. Calling him would also have been difficult, as his wife kept a close eye on him; she probably had spies stationed in all his various offices. A hint of suspicion and the whole thing would be undone: Shanghai crawled with potential informers, all of them eager to ingratiate themselves with the mighty Yi Taitai. And if Jiazhi had not pursued him so energetically, he might have cast her aside. Apartments were a popular parting gift to discarded mistresses of Wang Jingwei's ministers. He had too many temptations jostling before him; far too many for any one moment. And if one of them weren't kept constantly in view, it would slip to the

back, and then out, of his mind. No: he had to be nailed –
even if she had to keep his nose buried between her breasts
to do it.

'They weren't this big two years ago,' he had murmured to
her, in between kisses.

His head against her chest, he hadn't seen her blush.

Even now, it stung her to recall those knowing smirks – from
all of them, Kuang Yumin included. Only Liang Runsheng had
pretended not to notice how much bigger her breasts now
looked. Some episodes from her past she needed to keep
banished from her mind.

It was some distance to the foreign concessions. When the
pedicab reached the corner of Jing'an Temple and Seymour
roads, she told him to stop by a small café. She looked around
her, on the off chance that his car had already arrived. She could
see only a vehicle with a bulky, charcoal-burning tank parked a
little way up the street.

Most of the café's business must have been in take-out; there
were hardly any places to sit down inside. Towards the back of
its dingy interior was a refrigerated cabinet filled with various
Western-style cakes. A glaringly bright lamp in the passageway
behind exposed the rough, uneven surface of the brown paint
covering the lower half of the walls. A white military-style
uniform hung to one side of a small fridge; above, nearer the
ceiling, hung a row of long, lined gowns – like a rail in a second-
hand clothing store – worn by the establishment's Chinese
servants and waiters.

He had told her that the place had been opened by a Chinese
who had started out working in Tianjin's oldest, most famous
Western eatery, the Kiessling. He must have chosen this place,
she thought, because he would be unlikely to run into any
high-society acquaintances here. It was also situated on a main

road, so if he did bump into someone, it would not look as suspicious as if he were seen somewhere off the beaten track; it was central enough that one could plausibly be on one's way to somewhere entirely above-board.

She waited, the cup of coffee in front of her steadily losing heat. The last time, in the apartment, he had kept her waiting almost a whole hour. If the Chinese are the most unpunctual of people, she meditated, their politicians are surely virtuosos in the art of the late arrival. If she had to wait much longer, the store would be closed before they got there.

It had been his idea in the first place, after their first assignation. 'Let's buy you a ring to celebrate today – you choose it. I'd go with you myself, if I had the time.' Their second meeting was an even more rushed affair, and he had not mentioned it again. If he failed to remember today, she would have to think of artful ways of reminding him. With any other man, she would have made herself look undignified, grasping. But a cynical old fox like him would not delude himself that a pretty young woman would attach herself to a squat fifty-year-old merely for the beauty of his soul; a failure to express her material interest in the affair would seem suspicious. Ladies, in any case, are always partial to jewellery. She had, supposedly, travelled to Shanghai to trade in feminine luxuries. That she should try to generate a little extra profit along the way was entirely to be expected. As he was in the espionage business himself, he probably suspected conspiracies even where they didn't exist, where no cause for doubt had been given. Her priority was to win his trust, to appear credible. So far they had met in locations of his choosing; today she had to persuade him to follow her lead.

Last time he had sent the car on time to fetch her. The long wait she had had to endure today must mean he was coming himself. That was a relief: if they were due to tryst in an apartment, it would be hard to coax him out again once they were ensconced. Unless he had planned for them to stay out late together, to go out somewhere for dinner first – but he hadn't taken her to dinner on either of the previous two occasions. He would be wanting to take his time with her, while she would be getting jittery that the shop would close; but she wouldn't be able to hurry him along, like a prostitute with a customer.

She took out her powder compact and dabbed at her face. There was no guarantee he'd be coming to meet her himself. Now that the novelty had worn off, he was probably starting to lose interest. If she didn't pull it off today, she might not get another chance.

She glanced at her watch again. She felt a kind of chilling premonition of failure, like a long snag in a silk stocking, silently creeping up her body. On a seat a little over the way from hers, a man dressed in a Chinese robe – also on his own, reading a newspaper – was studying her. He'd been there when she had arrived, so he couldn't have been following her. Perhaps he was trying to guess what line of business she was in; whether her jewellery was real or fake. She didn't have the look of a dancing girl, but if she was an actress, he couldn't put a name to the face.

She had, in a past life, been an actress; and here she was, still playing a part, but in a drama too secret to make her famous.

While at college in Canton she'd starred in a string of rousingly patriotic history plays. Before the city fell to the Japanese, her university had relocated to Hong Kong, where the drama troupe had given one last public performance. Overexcited, unable to wind down after the curtain had fallen, she had gone out for a bite to eat with the rest of the cast. But even after almost everyone else had dispersed, she still hadn't wanted to go home. Instead, she and two female classmates had ridden through the city on the deserted upper deck of a tram as it swayed and trundled down the middle of the Hong Kong streets, the neon advertisements glowing in the darkness outside the windows.

Hong Kong University had lent a few of its classrooms to the Cantonese students, but lectures were always jam-packed, uncomfortably reminding them of their refugee status. The disappointing apathy of average Hong Kong people towards China's state of national emergency filled the classmates with a strong, indignant sense of exile, even though they had travelled little more than a hundred miles over the border to reach Hong Kong. Soon enough, a few like-minded elements among them formed a small radical group. When Wang Jingwei, soon to begin negotiating with the Japanese over forming a collabor-ationist government back on the Mainland, arrived on the island with his retinue of supporters – many of them also from near Canton – the students discovered that one of his aides came from the same town as Kuang Yumin. Exploiting this coinci-dence, Kuang sought him out and easily struck up a friendship, in the process extracting from him various items of useful information about members of Wang's group. After he had reported his findings to his co-conspirators, they resolved after much discussion to set a honey trap for one Mr Yee: to seduce him, with the help of one of their female classmates, towards an assassin's bullet. First she would befriend the wife, then move in on the husband. But if she presented herself as a student – always the most militant members of the population – Yi Taitai would be instantly on her guard. Instead, the group decided to make her the young wife of a local businessman; that sounded unthreatening enough, particularly in Hong Kong, where men of commerce were almost always apolitical. Enter the female star of the college drama troupe.

Of the various members of the group, Huang Lei was the wealthiest – from family money – and he briskly raised the funds to build a front for the conspiracy: renting a house, hiring a car, borrowing costumes. And since he was the only one of them able to drive, he took the part of chauffeur. Ouyang Lingwen was cast as the businessman husband, Mr Mai; Kuang Yumin as a cousin of the family, chaperoning the lovely Mai Taitai on her first meeting with Yi Taitai. After taking Kuang and the obligingly talkative aide back home, the car then drove the two ladies on to the Central District, to go about their shopping alone.

She had seen Mr Yi a few times, but only in passing. When they finally sat down in the same room together – the first time the Yis invited her to play mahjong with them – she could tell right away he was interested, despite his obvious attempts to be circumspect. Since the age of twelve or thirteen, she had been no stranger to the admiring male gaze. She knew the game. He was terrified of indiscretion, but at the same time finding his tediously quiet life in Hong Kong stifling. He didn't even dare drink, for fear the Wangs might summon him for duty at any moment. He and another member of the Wang clique had rented an old house together, inside which they remained cloistered, diverting themselves only with the occasional game of mahjong.

During the game, the conversation turned to the fabric Yi Taitai had bought to make suits for her husband. Jiazhi recommended a tailor who had done work for her in the past. 'He'll be rushed off his feet right now, with all the tourist trade, so it could take him a few months. But if Yi Taitai telephones me when Mr Yi has a free moment, I'll take him. He'll get them done faster if he knows it's for a friend of mine.' As she was going, she left her phone number on the table. While his wife was at the door, seeing Jiazhi out, Mr Yi would surely have time to copy it down for himself. Then, over the next couple of days, he could find an opportunity to call her – during office hours, when Mr Mai would be out at work. And they could take it from there.

That evening a light drizzle had been falling. Huang Lei drove her back home and they went back into the house together, where everybody was nervously waiting for news of the evening's triumph. Resplendent in the high-society costume in which she had performed so supremely, she wanted everyone to stay on to celebrate with her, to carouse with her until morning. None of the male students were dancers, but a bowl of soup at one of those small, all-night restaurants and a long walk through the damp night would do just as well. Anything to avoid bed.

Instead, a quiet gradually fell over the assembled company. There was whispering in a couple of corners, and secretive, tittering laughter; laughter she had heard before. They had been talking it over behind her back for some time, she realized.

'Apparently, Liang Runsheng is the only one who has any experience,' Lai Xiujin, the only other girl in the group, told her.

Liang Runsheng.

Of course. He was the only one who had been inside a brothel.

But given that she had already determined to make a sacrifice of herself, she couldn't very well resent him for being the only candidate for the job.

And that evening, while she basked in the heady afterglow of her success, even Liang Runsheng didn't seem quite as repellent as usual. One by one, the others saw the way the thing would go; one by one they slipped away, until the two of them were left alone. And so the show went on.

Days passed. Mr Yi did not call. In the end, she decided to telephone Yi Taitai, who sounded listless, offhand: she'd been too busy to go shopping in the last few days, but she'd give her another ring in a day or two.

Did Yi Taitai suspect something? Had she discovered her husband in possession of Jiazhi's phone number? Or had they had bad news from the Japanese? After two weeks tormented by worry, she finally received a jubilant phone call from Yi Taitai: to say goodbye. She was sorry they were in such a hurry that there'd be no time to meet before they left, but they would love to have her and her husband visit in Shanghai. They must come for a good long time, so they could all go on a trip to Nanjing together. Wang Jingwei's plan to go back to Nanjing to form a government must have temporarily run aground, Jiazhi speculated, and forced them to lie low for a while.

Huang Lei was by now in serious trouble, up to his eyes in debt. And when his family cut off his allowance on hearing that he was cohabiting with a dancing girl in Hong Kong, the scheme's finances collapsed.

The thing with Liang Runsheng had been awkward from the start; and now that she was so obviously regretting the whole business, the rest of the group began to avoid her. No one would look her in the eye.

'I was an idiot,' she said to herself, 'such an idiot.'

Had she been set up, she wondered, from the very beginning of this dead-end drama?

From this point on, she kept her distance not only from Liang Runsheng, but also from their entire little group. All the time she was with them, she felt they were eyeing her curiously – as if she were some kind of freak, or grotesque. After Pearl Harbor, the sea lanes reopened and all her classmates transferred to Shanghai. Although it, too, had been occupied by the Japanese, its colleges were still open; there was still an education (of sorts) to be had. She did not go with them, and did not try to find them when she got there herself.

For a long time, she agonized over whether she had caught something from Liang Runsheng.

Not long after reaching Shanghai, however, the students made contact with an underground worker called Wu – doubtless an alias – who, as soon as he heard about the high-ranking connection they had made, naturally encouraged them to pursue their scheme. And when they approached her, she resolved to do her duty and see the thing through.

In truth, every time she was with Yi she felt cleansed, as if by a scalding hot bath; for now everything she did was for the cause.

They must have posted someone to watch the entrance to the café, and alert everyone the instant his car drew up. When she'd arrived, she hadn't spotted anyone loitering about. The Ping'an Theatre directly opposite would have been an obvious choice, its corridor of pillars offering the perfect cover for a lookout. People were, in any case, always hanging around theatre entrances; one could easily wait there without arousing suspicion. But it was a little too far away to identify clearly the occupant of a car parked on the other side of the road.

A delivery bike, apparently broken down, was parked by the entrance to a leather-goods shop next door. Its owner – a man of around thirty, with a crew-cut – was bent over the mechanism, trying to repair it. Though she couldn't see his face clearly, she was fairly sure he wasn't someone she had seen before. She somehow doubted the bike was the getaway vehicle. There were some things they didn't tell her, and some she didn't ask. But she had heard that members of her old group had been chosen for the job. Even with Wu's help and connections, though, they might not have been able to get hold of a car for afterwards. If that car with a charcoal tank stayed where it was, parked just up from the café, it might turn out to be theirs. In which case it would be Huang Lei at the wheel. As she'd approached the café from behind the vehicle, she hadn't seen the driver.

She suspected that Wu didn't have much faith in them: he was probably afraid they were too inexperienced, that they'd get caught and fall to pieces in an interrogation, implicating other people in the process. Jiazhi was sure he was more than a one-man operation here in Shanghai, but he'd been Kuang Yumin's only point of contact throughout.

He'd promised to let them join his network. Maybe this was their test.

'Before they fire, they get so close the gun's almost up against the body,' Kuang Yumin had once told her, smiling. 'They don't shoot from a distance, like in the movies.'

This had probably been an attempt to reassure her that they wouldn't cut everyone around him down in an indiscriminate hail of fire. Even if she survived a bullet wound, it would cripple her for life. She'd rather die.

The moment had almost arrived, bringing with it a sharp taste of anticipation.

Her stage fright always evaporated once the curtain was up.

But this waiting was a torment. Men, at least, could smoke through their tension. Opening her handbag, she took out a small bottle of perfume and touched the stopper behind her ears. Its cool, glassy edge felt like her only point of contact with tangible reality. An instant later she caught the scent of Cape Jasmine.

She took off her coat and dabbed some more perfume in the crooks of her elbows. Before she'd had time to put it back on, she saw, through the tiers of a white display-model wedding cake in the window, a car parked outside the café. It was his.

She gathered up her coat and handbag, and walked out with them over her arm. By the time she approached, the driver had opened the door for her. Mr Yi was sitting in the middle of the back seat.

'I'm late, I know,' he muttered, stooping slightly in apology.

She sent him a long, accusing look, then got in. After the driver had returned to his seat, Mr Yi told him to drive to Ferguson Road – presumably to the apartment where their last assignation had taken place.

'I need to get to a jeweller's first,' she told him in a low voice. 'I want to replace a diamond stud that's fallen out of one of my earrings. There's a place just here. I would have gone before you got here, but I was afraid I might miss you. So I ended up waiting for ages on my own, like an idiot.'

He laughed. 'I'm sorry – just as I was leaving, a couple of people I needed to see showed up.' He leaned forward to speak to the chauffeur: 'Go back to where we just came from.' They had already driven some distance away.

'Everything's always so difficult,' she pouted. 'We're never private at home, there's never a chance to say a word to each other. I want to go back to Hong Kong. Can you get me a boat ticket?'

'Missing the husband?'

'Don't talk to me about him!'

She had told Mr Yi she was taking revenge for her husband's indiscretion with a dancing girl.

As they sat next to each other in the back of the car, he folded his arms so that his elbow nudged against the fullest part of her breast. This was a familiar trick of his: to sit primly upright while covertly enjoying the pleasurable softness of her.

She twisted around to look out the window, to tell the chauffeur exactly where to stop. The car made a U-turn at the next crossroads, and then another a little further on to get them back to the Ping'an, the only respectable second-run cinema in the city. The building's dull red façade curved inwards, like a sickle blade set upon the street corner. Opposite was Commander Kai's Café again, with the Siberian Leather Goods Store and the Green House Ladies' Clothing Emporium next, each fronted by two large display windows filled with glamorously dressed mannequins bent into all manner of poses beneath neon signs. The next-door establishment was smaller and far more nondescript. Although the sign over the door said JEWELLER'S, its single display window was empty.

He told the chauffeur to stop the car, then got out and followed her inside. Though, in her high-heeled shoes, she was half a head taller than him, he clearly did not mind the disparity in their heights. Tall men, she had found in her experience, liked girls who were small, while short men seemed to prefer their women to tower over them – perhaps out of a desire for balance. She knew he was watching her, and so slightly exaggerated the swivel of her hips as she sashayed through the glass doors like a sea dragon.

An Indian dressed in a Western-style suit greeted them. Though the shop was small, its interior was light, high-ceilinged, and almost entirely bare. It was fitted out with just one waist-high glass showcase, towards the back, in which were displayed some birthstones, one for each month of the year –

semi-precious yellow quartz, or red or blue gems made of sapphire or ruby dust, supposed to bring good luck.

She took out of her bag a pear-shaped ruby earring, at the top of which a diamond-studded leaf was missing one stone.

'We can get one to match it,' the Indian said, after taking a look.

When she asked how much it would cost and when it would be ready, Mr Yi added: 'Ask him if he has any decent rings.' As he had chosen to study in Japan, rather than Britain or the United States, he felt uncomfortable speaking English and always got other people to interpret for him.

She hesitated. 'Why?'

He smiled. 'I said I wanted to buy you a ring, didn't I? A diamond ring – a decent one.'

After another pause, she gave an almost stoic, resigned smile, then softly asked: 'Do you have any diamond rings?'

The Indian shouted a startling, incomprehensible stream of what sounded like Hindi upstairs, then escorted them up.

To one side of the cream-coloured back wall of the showroom was a door leading to a pitch-dark staircase. The office was on a little mezzanine set between the two floors of the building, with a shallow balcony overlooking the shop floor – presumably for surveillance purposes. The wall immediately to their left as they entered was hung with two mirrors of different sizes, each painted with multicoloured birds and flowers and inscribed with gilded Chinese calligraphy: THIS ROC WILL SURELY SOAR TEN THOUSAND MILES. CONGRATULATIONS, MR BADA, ON YOUR GRAND OPENING. RESPECTFULLY, CHEN MAOKUN. Too tall for the room's sloping ceiling, a third large mirror, decorated with a phoenix and peonies, had been propped up against another wall.

To the front of the room, a desk had been placed along the

ebony railing, with a telephone and a reading lamp resting on top. Next to it was a tea table on which sat a typewriter, covered with an old piece of glazed cloth. A second, squat Indian, with a broad ashen-brown face and a nose squashed like a lion's muzzle, stood up from his round-backed armchair to move chairs over for them.

'So it is diamond rings you are interested in. Sit down, please, sit down.' He waddled slowly off to a corner of the room, his stomach visibly preceding him, then bent over a low green, ancient-looking safe.

This, clearly, was not a high-class establishment. Though Mr Yi appeared unfazed by his dingy surroundings, Jiazhi felt a twinge of embarrassment that she had brought him here. These days, she'd heard, some shops were just a front for black marketers or speculators.

Wu had selected this store for its proximity to Commander Kai's Café. As she'd walked up the stairs, it had occurred to her that on his way back down they would catch him as easily as a turtle in a jar. As he would probably insist on walking in front of her, he would step first into the showroom. There, a couple of male customers browsing the display cabinet would suddenly move out to block his way. But two men couldn't spend too long pretending to choose cheap cuff-links, tie pins and trinkets for absent lady-friends; they couldn't dawdle indecisively like girls. Their entrance needed to be perfectly timed: neither too late nor too early. And once they were in, they had to stay in. Patrolling up and down outside was not an option; his chauffeur would quickly get suspicious. Their best delaying tactic was probably gazing at the window display of the leather shop next door, several yards behind the car.

Sitting to one side of the desk, she couldn't help turning to look down over the balcony. Only the shop window fell within her line of vision. As the window was clear and its glass shelves empty, she could see straight out to the pavement, and to the edge of the car parked next to it.

Then again, perhaps two men shopping alone would look far too conspicuous. They might draw the attention not only of the chauffeur, but also of Mr Yi himself, from the balcony upstairs, who might then grow suspicious and delay his return downstairs. A stalemate would be catastrophic. Perhaps they would catch him instead at the entrance to the shop. In which case their timing would need to be even more perfect. They would need to approach at a walk, as the sound of running footsteps would instantly alert the chauffeur. Mr Yi had brought only his driver with him, so perhaps the latter was doubling as a bodyguard.

Or maybe the two of them would split up, one of them lingering in front of the Green House Ladies' Clothing Emporium arm in arm with Lai Xiujin, her eyes glued to the window display. A girl could stand for minutes on end staring at clothes she couldn't afford, while her boyfriend waited impatiently, his back to the shop window, looking around him.

All these scenarios danced vaguely through her mind, even as she realized that none of this was her concern. She could not lose the feeling that, upstairs in this little shop, she was sitting on top of a powder keg that was about to blow her sky-high. A slight tremble was beginning to take hold of her legs.

The shop assistant had gone back downstairs. The boss was much darker skinned than his assistant; they did not look to be father and son. The younger man had saggy, stubbled, pouch-like cheeks and heavy-lidded, sleepy-looking eyes. Though not tall, he was built sturdily enough to serve, if necessity arose, as security guard. The position of the jewellery cabinet so near the back of the shop and the bare window display suggested that they were afraid of being robbed, even in daylight; a padlock hung by the door, for use at night. So there must be something of value on the premises: probably gold bars, US dollars and silver.

She watched as the Indian brought out a black velvet tray, around a foot long, inlaid with rows of diamond rings. She and Mr Yi leaned in.

Seeing their lack of interest – neither picked one up to have a closer look – the proprietor put the tray back in the safe. 'I've this one, too,' he added, opening a small blue velvet box. Set deep within was a pink diamond, the size of a pea.

No one was selling pink diamonds at the moment, she remembered Yi Taitai saying. After her initial astonishment had passed, she felt a rush of relief – that the shop had, in the end, come through for her. Until the pink diamond, she had looked like an incompetent bounty-hunter, a Cantonese nobody dragging her powerful Shanghai sugar daddy to a tatty gemstone boutique. Of course, the moment the gun sounded, everything – including all peripheral thoughts of plausibility, of pride – would shatter. Although she understood this well enough, she could not allow herself to think about it, for fear that he would see the terror on her face.

She picked up the ring. He laughed softly as he looked at the stone in her hand: 'Now that's more like it.' She felt a numb chill creeping up the back of her head; the display windows downstairs and the glass door between them seemed to be broadening out, growing taller, as if behind her were an enormous, two-storey-high expanse of brilliant, fragile glass, ready to disintegrate at any moment. But even as she felt almost dizzy with the precariousness of her situation, the shop seemed to be blanketing her in torpor. Inside she could hear only the muffled buzz of the city outside – because of the war, there were far fewer cars on the road than usual; the sounding of a horn was a rarity. The warm, sweet air inside the office pressed soporifically down on her like a quilt. Though she was vaguely aware that something was about to happen, her heavy head was telling her that it must all be a dream.

She examined the ring under the lamplight, turning it over in her fingers. Sitting by the balcony, she began to imagine that the bright windows and door visible behind her were a cinema screen across which an action movie was being shown. She had always hated violent films; as a child, she had turned her back whenever a scene became grisly.

'Six carats. Try it on,' the Indian urged.

She decided to enjoy the drowsy intimacy of this jeweller's den. Her eyes flitted to the reflection of her foot, nestling amid clumps of peonies, in the mirror propped against the wall, then back to the fabulous treasure – worthy, surely, of a tale from the *Thousand and One Nights* – on her finger. She turned the ring this way, then that, comparing it to the rose red of her nail varnish. Though it seemed pale and small next to her brightly lacquered nails, inside the gloomy office it had an alluring sparkle, like a star burning pink in dusk light. She registered a twinge of regret that it was to be no more than a prop in the short, penultimate scene of the drama unfolding around it.

'So what do you think?' Mr Yi said.

'What do you think?'

'I'm no expert. I'm happy if you like it.'

'Six carats. I don't know whether there are any faults in it. I can't see any.'

They leaned in together over the ring, talking and laughing like an engaged couple. Although she had been educated in Canton, the earliest treaty port to open to British traders, the schools there had not attached as much importance to teaching English as they did in Hong Kong, and she always spoke the language in timid, low tones. Sensing her lack of linguistic confidence, the proprietor decided to spare her his usual negotiating preamble on the whys-and-wherefores of diamond-costing. A price was quickly agreed upon: eleven gold bars, to be delivered tomorrow. If any individual bars turned out to fall below the regulation weight, Mr Yi pledged to make up the difference; likewise, the jeweller promised to reimburse them for any that were too heavy. The entire transaction – trading gold for diamonds – felt like another detail stolen from the *Thousand and One Nights*.

She worried that the whole thing had been wrapped up too quickly. They probably weren't expecting her and Yi to re-emerge so soon. Dialogue, she knew, was the best filler of stage time.

'Shall we ask for a receipt?' He would probably be thinking of sending someone over tomorrow, to deliver the gold and pick up the ring.

The Indian was already writing one out. The ring had also been taken off and returned to him.

They sat back next to each other in their chairs, relaxing in the post-negotiation détente.

She laughed softly. 'These days no one wants anything but gold. They don't even want a cash deposit.'

'Just as well. I never carry any on me.'

She knew, from her experience of living with the Yis, that it was always the aides who covered incidental costs – it was a minister's privilege never to dig into his own pockets. Today, of course, he had come out alone, and therefore penniless, because of the need for secrecy.

The English say that power is an aphrodisiac. She didn't

know whether this was true; she herself was entirely oblivious to its attractions. They also say that the way to a man's heart is through his stomach; that a man will fall easy prey to a woman who can cook. Somewhere in the first decade or two of the twentieth century, a well-known Chinese scholar was supposed to have added that the way to a woman's heart is through her vagina. Though his name escaped her, she could remember the analogy he had devised in defence of male polygamy: 'A teapot is always surrounded by more than one cup.'

She refused to believe that an intellectual would come out with something so vulgar. Nor did she believe the saying was true, except perhaps for desperate old prostitutes or merry widows. In her case, she had found Liang Runsheng repellent enough before the whole thing began, and afterwards even more so.

Though maybe that was not a valid example, because Liang Runsheng had been anxious, insecure, painfully aware of her dislike from the outset. His obvious sense of inferiority only grew as things went along between them, increasing her contempt for him.

Surely she hadn't fallen in love with Yi? Despite her fierce scepticism towards the idea, she found herself unable to refute the notion entirely; since she had never been in love, she had no idea what it might feel like. Because, since her mid-teens, she had been fully occupied in repelling romantic offensives, she had built up a powerful resistance to forming emotional attachments. For a time, she had thought she might be falling for Kuang Yumin, but she ended up hating him – for turning out just like the others.

The two occasions she had been with Yi, she had been so tense, so taken up in saying her lines that there had been no opportunity to ask herself how she actually felt. At the house, she had to be constantly on her guard. Every night she was expected to stay up socializing as late as everyone else. When she was finally released back to the privacy of her own room, she would gulp down a sleeping pill to guarantee herself a good night's sleep. Though Kuang Yumin had given her a small bottle of them, he had told her to avoid taking them if she possibly could, in case anything were to happen in the morning for which a clear head would be required. But without them, she was tormented by insomnia, something she had never suffered from in the past.

Only now, as this last, tense moment of calm stretched infinitely out, on this cramped balcony, the artificial brightness of its lamplight contrasting grubbily with the pale sky visible through the door and windows downstairs, could she permit herself to relax and inquire into her own feelings. Somehow, the nearby presence of the Indian, bent over his writing desk, only intensified her sense of being entirely alone with her lover. But now was not the moment to ask herself whether she loved him; instead, she needed to –

He was gazing off into the middle distance, a faintly sorrowful smile on his face. He had never dared dream such happiness would come his way in middle age. It was, of course, his power and position that he had principally to thank; they were an inseparable part of him. Presents, too, were essential, though they needed to be distributed at the correct moments. Given too soon, they carried within an insulting insinuation of greed. Though he knew perfectly well the rules of the game they were playing, he had to permit himself a brief moment of euphoria at the prize that had fallen into his lap; otherwise, the entire exercise was meaningless.

He was an old hand at this: taking his paramours shopping, ministering to their whims, retreating into the background while they made their choices. But there was, she noted again, no cynicism in his smile just then; only sadness. He sat in silhouette against the lamp, seemingly sunk into an attitude of tenderly affectionate contemplation, his downcast eyelashes tinged the dull cream of moths' wings as they rested on his gaunt cheeks.

He really loves me, she thought. Inside, she felt a raw tremor of shock – then a vague sense of loss.

It was too late.

The Indian passed the receipt to him. He placed it inside his jacket.

'Run,' she said softly.

For a moment he stared, and then understood everything. Springing up, he barged the door open, steadied himself on the frame, then swung down to grab firm hold of the banister and stumbled down the dark, narrow stairs. She heard his footsteps break into a run, taking the stairs two or three at a time, thudding irregularly over the treads.

Too late. She had realized too late.

The jeweller was obviously bewildered. Conscious of how suspicious their behaviour must look, she forced herself to sit still, resisting the temptation to look down.

They listened to the sound of shoes pounding on floor tiles until he burst into their line of vision, shooting out of the glass door like a cannonball. A moment later, the burly shop assistant also emerged into view, following close behind. She was terrified he might attempt to pull Yi back and ask him to explain himself; a delay of even a few seconds would be fatal. Intimidated, perhaps, by the sight of the official car, however, the Indian stopped in the store entrance, staring out, his heavy, muscular silhouette blocking the doorway. After that, all they heard was the screech of an engine, as if the vehicle were rearing up on its back wheels, followed by a bang. The slam of a door, perhaps – or a gunshot? Then the car roared off.

If it had been gunfire, they would have heard more than one shot.

She steadied herself. Quiet returned.

She heaved a sigh of relief; her entire body felt weak, exhausted, as if just recovered from serious illness. Carefully gathering up her coat and handbag, she smiled and nodded as she got up from her chair: 'Tomorrow, then.' She lowered her voice again, to its normal English-speaking mumble. 'He'd forgotten about another appointment, so he needed to hurry.'

The jeweller had already taken his eyeglass back out and adjusted the focus to ascertain that the gentleman just left had not first swapped the pink diamond ring for another. He then saw her smilingly out.

She couldn't blame him for wanting to make sure. The negotiations over price had been suspiciously brief and easy.

She hurried down the stairs. When the shop assistant saw her reappear he hesitated, then seemed to decide to say nothing. As she left, however, she heard shouting between upstairs and down.

There were no free pedicabs outside the shop, so she walked on towards Seymour Road. The group surely must have scattered the moment they saw him dash for the car and drive off; they would have realized that the game was up. She couldn't relax; what if someone had been assigned to watch the back door? What if he hadn't seen what had happened at the front, and hadn't yet left the scene? What would happen if she ran into him? But even if he suspected her of treachery, he wouldn't confront her there and then, much less summarily execute her.

She felt surprised that it was still light outside, as if inside the store she had lost all sense of time. The pavement around her was heaving with humanity; pedicab after pedicab rushed past on the road, all of them taken. Pedestrians and vehicles flowed on by, as if separated from her by a wall of glass, and no more accessible than the elegant mannequins in the window of the Green House Ladies' Clothing Emporium – you could look, but you couldn't touch. They glided along, imperviously serene, as she stood on the outside, alone in her agitation.

She was on the watch for a charcoal-fired vehicle drawing suddenly up beside her, and for a hand darting out to pull her inside.

The pavement in front of the Ping'an Theatre was deserted: the audience was not yet spilling out at the end of a show, so no pedicabs were lined up outside, waiting for customers. Just as she was hesitating over which direction to walk in, she turned and saw that some distance away, along the opposite side of the street, an empty pedicab was slowly approaching, a red, green and white windmill tied to its handlebar. Seeing her wave and shout at him, the tall young cyclist hurried to cross over, the little windmill spinning faster as he accelerated towards her.

'Yu Garden Road,' she told him as she got in.

Fortunately, while she'd been in Shanghai she'd had very little direct contact with the group, and so had never got around to mentioning that she had a relative living on Yu Garden Road. She thought she would stay there a few days, while she assessed the situation.

As the pedicab approached Jing'an Temple, she heard a whistle blow.

'The road's blocked,' her cyclist told her.

A middle-aged man in a short jacket was pulling a length of rope across the street, holding the whistle in his mouth. On the other side of the road, a second, similarly dressed man pulled the other end of the rope straight to seal off the traffic and pedestrians within. Someone was lethargically ringing a bell, the thin, tinny sound barely carrying over the wide street.

Her pedicab driver cycled indomitably up to the rope, then braked and impatiently spun his windmill, before turning around to smile at her.

Three black capes were now sitting around the mahjong table. The nose of the new arrival – Liao Taitai – was speckled with white pockmarks.

'Mr Yi,' back,' Ma Taitai smirked.

'What a wicked liar that Wang Jiazhi is!' Yi Taitai complained. 'Promising to take us all out to dinner then running away. I'll collapse with hunger if she makes us wait much longer!'

'Mr Yi,' Liao Taitai smiled. 'Your wife's bankrupted us all today. She'll be the one buying dinner tomorrow.'

'Mr Yi,' Ma Taitai said, 'where's the dinner you promised us last time you won? It's impossible to get a meal out of you.'

'Mr Yi ought to buy us dinner tonight, since we can never get him to accept our invitations,' the other black cape said.

He merely smiled. After the maid brought him tea, he knocked his cigarette ash on to the saucer, glancing across at the thick wool curtains covering the wall opposite and wondering how many assassins they could conceal. He was still shaken by the afternoon's events.

Tomorrow he must remember to have them taken down, though his wife was bound to object to something so expensive being sidelined into a storeroom.

It was all her fault, the result of her careless choice of friends. But even he was impressed by how elaborately, how far in advance – two years – the entire trap had been premeditated. The preparations had, indeed, been so perfectly thorough that

33

only a last-minute change of heart on the part of his *femme fatale* had saved him. So she really had loved him – his first true love. What a stroke of luck.

He could have kept her on. He had heard or read somewhere that all spies are brothers; that they can feel a loyalty to one another stronger than the causes that divide them. In any case, she was only a student. Of that group of theirs, only one had been in the pay of Chongqing, the one who had gotten away – the single glitch in the entire operation. Most likely he'd stepped out of the Ping'an halfway through a showing, then gone back into the theatre once the assassination attempt was aborted. After the area was sealed off, he would have shown the police his ticket stub and then been allowed to slip away. The young man who'd waited with him to do the job had seen him check that the stub was safely stashed along with his cigarettes. It had been agreed in advance that he wouldn't take up room in the getaway car; that afterwards he would stroll inconspicuously back into the cinema. After they'd been roughed up a bit, the little idiots came out with the whole story.

Mr Yi stood behind his wife, watching the game. After he had stubbed out his cigarette, he took a sip of his tea; still too hot. Though an early night was surely what he needed, he was overtired, unable to wind down. He was exhausted from sitting by the phone all afternoon waiting for news; he hadn't even had a proper dinner. As soon as he'd reached safety, he'd immediately telephoned to get the whole area sealed off. By ten o'clock that evening they'd all been shot. She must have hated him at the end. But real men have to be ruthless. She wouldn't have loved him if he'd been the sentimental type.

And, of course, his hands had been tied – more by Zhou Fohai than by the Japanese military police. For some time Zhou had been directing his own secret-service operation, and saw

Government Intelligence – Mr Yi's department – as an irrelevance. Consequently, he kept an oppressively close eye on them, always on the lookout for evidence of incompetence. Mr Yi could imagine all too easily what use Zhou would have made of the discovery that the head of Domestic Intelligence had given house-room to an assassin's plant.

Now, at least, Zhou could find no grounds on which to reproach him. If he accused him of executing potentially useful witnesses, he could confidently counter that they'd been only students; they weren't experienced spies from whom a slow, reasoned torture could have spilled useful information. And if the executions had been delayed, word of the affair might have gotten out. They would have become patriotic heroes plotting to assassinate a national traitor; a rallying point for popular discontent.

He was not optimistic about the way the war was going, and he had no idea how it would turn out for him. But now that he had enjoyed the love of a beautiful woman, he could die happy – without regret. He could feel her shadow forever near him, comforting him. Even though she had hated him at the end, she had at least felt something. And now he possessed her utterly, primitively – as a hunter does his quarry, a tiger his kill. Alive, her body belonged to him; dead, she was his ghost.

'Take us out to dinner, Mr Yi! Take us out!' the three black capes chirruped ferociously. 'He promised last time!'

'So did Ma Taitai,' Yi Taitai smilingly intervened, 'then when we didn't see her for a few days, we forgot all about it.'

'Ever the loyal wife,' Ma Taitai smiled back.

'Look, is Mr Yi going to take us to dinner or not?'

'Mr Yi has certainly had a run of luck lately,' Ma Taitai pronounced, looking at him and smiling again. They understood each other perfectly. She could hardly have failed to notice the two of them disappearing, one after the other. And the girl still wasn't back. He had looked distracted when he returned, the elation still glimmering over his face. This afternoon, she guessed, had been their first assignation.

He reminded himself to drill his wife on the official story he had made up: that Mai Taitai had needed to hurry back to Hong Kong to take care of urgent family business. Then, to frighten her a bit with some secret-service patter: that not long after she invited this viper into the bosom of their home, he had received intelligence that she was part of a Chongqing spy ring. Just as his people had begun to make further inquiries, he had heard that the Japanese had gotten wind of it. If he hadn't struck first, he would have gotten none of the credit for the intelligence work already done, and the Japanese might have discovered the connection with his wife, and tried to incriminate him. Best lay it on thick, so that she didn't listen to Ma Taitai's gossip.

'Take us to dinner, Mr Yi! Stop getting your wife to do your dirty work.'

'My wife gives her own dinners. She's promised you tomorrow.'

'We know how busy you are, Mr Yi. You tell us when you're free, and we'll be there; any day after tomorrow.'

'No, take us tonight. How about Laixi?'

'The only edible thing there is the cold buffet.'

'German food is boring – nothing but cold cuts. How about somewhere Hunanese, just for a change?'

'Or there's Shuyu – Ma Taitai didn't come with us yesterday.'

'I'd rather Jiuru – I haven't been there for ages.'

'Didn't Yang Taitai hold a dinner at Jiuru?'

'Last time we went, we didn't have Liao Taitai with us. We needed someone from Hunan – we didn't know what to order.'

'It's too spicy for me!'

'Then tell the chef to make it less spicy.'

'Only cold fish won't eat hot chilli!'

Amid the raucous laughter, he quietly slipped out.

*Translated by Julia Lovell*

IN THE WAITING ROOM

At Pang Songling's bone-setting massage clinic, the waiting room was full. Behind the white partition, a man yelped in pain: 'Aiyo-wah! Aiyo-o-WAH! Not this time, Mr Pang, not just now – next time, please –'

Mr Pang chuckled. He was reciting his prescriptions, the rhythmic formulae of his art; his chanting made the words dense and heavy, like amber beads on a Buddhist rosary, with a whiff of old lady's sitting room – an ancient, grateful peace prayer. Added to this were some explanations of the spinal and nervous systems, all very scientific. He had a cut-away diagram of the human body, taken from Western medicine, posted on the wall, along with a Chinese medical licence issued by the Public Health Bureau, in a glass frame, complete with a two-inch ID photo taken thirty years ago. The patient's cries of pain gradually died out – then suddenly he gasped again: 'Aiyo!'

The ladies in the waiting room chuckled too, when they heard that. A maid kept patting the child that she held on her lap, afraid that he would cry. 'Don't cry, don't cry – we'll go get some steamed crab rolls, in just a little while!' The child, who had no intention of crying, sat on her lap like a sickly lump of lard. He wore split-crotch pants in a tiny floral pattern, and red-and-grey-striped woollen socks. Bulging out between pants and socks was the congealed flesh of little white legs. He turned to look at the maid, then came out with something quite surprising, for a child who was just five or so: 'Let's not get steamed rolls. Steamed rolls are never any good.' Based, it seemed, on extensive experience, as if he often dealt with this very question: 'So – how about steamed crab rolls, eh?' But the maid just glowered at him; one sharp glance and she went back, churlishly, to her own thoughts.

Mr Pang was telling his patient, Mr Gao, about the situation out on the streets: 'Things have gotten really bad these days! When a pedicab driver crosses the bridge, the police charge him ten dollars. And if he refuses? Why then, he's hauled off to the station. A driver rents a cab for half a day, you know. He has to earn enough, in half a day, to support himself and his family. Getting hauled off to the station, waiting around for two or three hours – even if it's all cleared up, and he's released, charges dismissed – he can't afford that. So it's goodbye, ten dollars – if you don't pay now, you'll just pay more later on.'

Pang Songling talked like a man in the know, here in occupied Shanghai. His melancholic remarks were laced with irony, and he was always making passing reference to his close relations with big officials: 'But the cops know what's out of bounds – if the cab is from the magistrate's office, they let it right through. Magistrate Zhu sends his pedicab for me every day, and that cab's never been stopped –'

Mrs Pang cut in, from the other side of the partition: 'They've got sharp eyes, those cops!' She had sharp eyes too, big eyes set in dark sockets, like a pair of bright lamps in her thin dark face. She sat hunched over the sweater she was knitting, a scrawny woman in a brown, shrunken sweater. She sat in the clinic all day long, nodding and smiling her buck-toothed smile at the patients as they came and went, or – when the greeting was perfunctory – simply baring her buck-teeth at them. This husband of hers did bear watching, now that this streak of success had him constantly running off to the homes of top officials.

Their daughter, Ah Fang, sat at the registration table counting up the money. Ah Fang was a tall girl, but she had buck-teeth too, and smiling eyes that were black and bright, in a concave, wok-bottom face. Every day she wore a dress of black-and-red-checked imitation wool, so big it was baggy on her, and a pair of homemade, grey cloth shoes. She had a lot of siblings, so she wouldn't get any pretty clothes until she had a likely match – but since she didn't have anything pretty to wear, she couldn't get a match. She was trapped in a vicious circle, doomed to spend her blooming years in wistful longing: no young woman, no matter how clever, could break her way out of a dress like that.

Mrs Pang looked at the soup plate sitting on that tired little table. 'Songling!' she called out in dismay. 'Your soup dumplings are getting cold.' There was no reply. 'Songling!' she called again. 'After you've finished this one, come and eat. The food's getting cold.'

Her husband acceded with a grunt, and went on talking seriously with his patient.

'"There is enough to go around" – that's what Mr Zhu said. I raised this question with him, and just like that he said: "There is enough to go around."

'That Magistrate Zhu,' Mr Pang went on, 'is someone I admire for two reasons. What two reasons, you may ask.'

Pang Songling had a yellowish, leonine face, so big and broad and stoutly joined to his neck that it resembled, from the front as from the back, a fat man's knee. He'd been a man of consequence since long before the war – officials came and went, but he held on to his position. And so his praise of Mr Zhu was measured, carefully thought out. He looked at the floor, and spoke in weighty, assured phrases: 'What two reasons? First, no matter how busy he is, he always goes to bed at eight o'clock. And the minute his head touches the pillow, he's out. Over the course of a day, the body gets tired and its cells are destroyed, but sleep resuscitates them. Mr Zhu has grasped this basic medical principle, and that's why he can stay full of energy, even with his busy schedule!'

Mr Pang was practically chewing his words, sucking on each one, feeling their sweetness in his mouth. He fell silent then, and worked his mouth hard, as if he were trying to dislodge a piece of gum that had gotten stuck against his teeth. He was weighing the merits of Mr Zhu, he had to give the man his due. 'And the other reason. Every day, after lunch, he studies for two hours. The first hour is for Chinese – classical Chinese, Confucian texts, and so on. The second hour is for modern subjects, like physics, geography, and foreign books in translation. He's hired a tutor, and that tutor, he's a learned man – he even has a wife who's learned too. Now *that* is something, eh?'

Here the conversation came to an end. 'Ah Fang,' the masseur called out, still kneading his patient, 'who's next?'

Ah Fang looked at the register. 'Mrs Wang.'

Mr Gao was in his short gown and knitted vest. His concubine hastened out, fetched his long outer gown from the clothes hook, and helped him into it, doing all the buttons for him. Then, after unhooking his cane, she used it to snag the wool hat from its perch – she had to do it that way, she was so short. She moved with deft, well-practised ease: a concubine of the old school, in her thirties, small and thin in her dowdy old padded gown of worn black silk, so long it brushed her feet. She had a squarish face, the cheeks lightly daubed with rouge, eyes that were hooded by thick upper lids, and a lowly, downward-turned gaze. She carefully put his hat on for him, using both hands. Then she rushed over to the teacup that was on the table, took a sip and tested it, and handed it to him. While he was drinking his tea, she reached into his inner pocket and took out a leather wallet. She counted out the money, and put a little stack of banknotes on the table.

Mrs Pang looked up and said, 'Oh, Mr Gao, are you leaving now?'

Mr Gao nodded. As they went out, the concubine was all manners: 'Goodbye, Mr Pang! See you tomorrow, Mrs Pang! See you tomorrow, Miss Pang, and see you tomorrow, Mrs Bao and Mrs Xi!' The women ignored her.

Pang Songling came out and washed his hands at the wash-stand near the door. He was wearing a jacket and pants made of soft silk, dull blue in colour. He propped one foot on his daughter's chair, picked up the soup plate, took his cigarette from his mouth, handed it to his wife, and started to eat. Mrs Pang smoked the cigarette and then, when he had finished eating, returned it to him. Neither one said a word.

Mrs Wang took off her coat and hung it on the hook, then undid her collar button. She sat on the rosewood bench inside the partition, waiting for her massage. 'Mrs Wang,' said Mrs Pang, 'did you have this coat made last year? I remember this wool fabric looked quite coarse then, but it's holding up well. Nowadays, everything is just so shoddy.'

There being no suitably modest way to reply to this, Mrs Wang merely smiled and nodded. The other women, though, they chimed right in. Never mind that it had been quite a while since any of them had bought new clothes; they were happy to complain about quality and price any time.

Mrs Xi's egg-shaped face had a pinkish-purple tinge, and her eyebrows were lightly sketched, her wrinkles faint, her bangs wispy – she'd cut her hair short, but hadn't permed it. She was wearing a short coat, soft green in colour. It was made of imitation wool, so she was emphatic: 'That's just how it is these days – even if you've got a purse full of money, you still can't find anything that looks halfway decent. It's not a question of price alone!' She reached into her blue-and-white mesh bag, took out her leather purse and flipped it back and forth in her hand, smiling.

'Anything that's halfway decent costs somewhere in the tens of thousands,' Mrs Pang put in. 'And if it's ugly – it's still up there in the thousands!'

Ah Fang locked her drawer, then slipped the keys into her underarm button loop for safekeeping as she walked across the room. She sat down next to Mrs Xi and said, with a smile, 'Mrs Xi, I've heard that your husband is doing very well up there in the interior.'

The sudden attention made Mrs Xi blush. 'Yes, he's doing quite well – he's the head of the branch office now. Things are still very hard, though. He can't send money back to Shanghai from Chongqing, so here I am, just barely scraping by.'

Ah Fang smiled her dark eye-socket smile, reached across to still the keys that jingled under her arm, and leaned closer to Mrs Xi. 'Maybe,' she said, keeping her voice low, 'your husband has another woman there!'

Mrs Xi thrust her fingers through the loops of her blue-and-white mesh bag, gave her knee a few pats, and sighed. 'Oh, Miss Pang – don't I know it! I've thought for a long time now that he must have taken a concubine. Once a man's been away for six months, you can't count on him any more. That's what I've always said!'

'If only you'd gone with him – then this never would have happened!' Ah Fang declared, nodding her head confidentially and smiling her secret, dark-eyed smile.

'I did go with him at first, to Hong Kong, but he got a telegram ordering him to Chongqing. He had to go by aeroplane, so I was to join him later, taking my time and getting there when I could. Who'd have guessed that getting out of Shanghai would suddenly become next to impossible? Well, when it comes to men, there's just not much you can rely on – still, here's something you would never imagine –' Mrs Xi pulled out a newspaper and slapped it hard against the sofa. 'They're telling the men to take another! The war's led to a drop in the population, they want the birth rate to rise, so they've gone and told the men that if they've been apart from their wives for two years, they can take another. And they're not even calling them concubines – they're calling them "second wives"! The commanders in Chongqing think the civil servants won't be able to focus on their work, unless they have someone to look after them. So they're telling the men to take another wife!'

'What did your parents-in-law say?'

'Oh, they let him do whatever he wants. What they said to me was, "Anyway, you'll always be the first wife." But I know what's up. After all, I'm in my forties now –'

'No – not really? You look barely thirty.'

'Oh, I'm old already!' Mrs Xi sighed. Then her doubt turned real, and forceful. 'I really have gotten old, haven't I?'

Ah Fang surveyed her critically. 'It's because you don't dress up the way you used to.'

Mrs Xi leaned forward, closer to Ah Fang. 'No,' she said softly. 'It's my hair. It's falling out by the handful.'

Everyone in the room heard what she said, which was fine with her; it made her afflictions gratifying. She grabbed the mesh bag in her fist and waved it in the air. 'You can't imagine what goes on, up there in the interior – a man gets promoted, and people just throw themselves at him! Really – they throw themselves at him!'

Mrs Wang was being massaged. Her head was thrust forward, her collar unbuttoned. A woman in her fifties, with a round, white, childlike face – her mouth held a steady smile, the tranquillity of little alleyways, off the major streets. Mr Pang thought he knew how to approach anyone, thought he had the common touch. 'So – are you still in that little alley?' he asked. Mrs Wang was startled. 'Uh-huh,' she replied.

'A new pharmacy just opened there, right?'

A vague mist suddenly descended on Mrs Wang's alley. All she could remember was a cobbler's shop across the way, in the dark and damp; the cobbler was a youngish man, and he did wear metal-rimmed glasses, but there was no sign of a pharmacy. Her smile faded a bit and she blinked wordlessly.

'I went by one day,' Mr Pang kept going, 'and I saw a new pharmacy. I thought it was right at the entrance to your alley.' His voice grew cold when he spoke of the pharmacist, who was after all a professional rival.

Mrs Wang thought he was angry with her, and she panicked. She gathered her wits, and tried to change the topic. 'We had a thief in our neighbourhood the other day.' But it felt far away, minuscule, even to her.

'Haven't you got a policeman to patrol your alley?' Mrs Pang demanded.

'Yes, yes, we do.'

Mr Pang left it at that. Mrs Wang's head pushed further and further forward, in response to the masseur's kneading. A steady little smile came to her face again – that dim, dark peace of the alleyways.

In came another countrified lady, also in her fifties, with thin black hair pulled into a topknot. She must have been a fortune-favoured beauty in her youth, her face was so round; but now that she'd put on weight, she seemed flabby and foolish. Her whole nebulous person was held in place by the supporting force of her jewelled hairpin, which was shaped like a sprig of red tassel-flower; and her earrings, which were bits of jade the size of mung beans; and two gold teeth. She was carrying a little girl, and she walked straight in, right to the partition, and greeted Mr Pang.

'Mrs Tong, please take a seat!' the masseur's wife called out hastily. 'Come take a seat out here!' She patted the chair next to her.

Mrs Tong, however, was a plain-spoken woman who always thought she should get special treatment. 'Mrs Pang, could you put me next?' She was still standing by the partition. 'I have to take this granddaughter of mine to the dentist. She's been teething, and it keeps us up all night.'

The reply she got came in a lazy manner. 'Just got here myself, so I don't know what's going on. Ah Fang, how many are there still?'

'Oh, not many at all. Please take a seat, Mrs Tong.'

'What's the time? The dentist closes up at half past one.'

'Plenty of time, plenty of time,' Ah Fang soothed.

The sofa was already full of people, but Mrs Tong said, 'Excuse me' and, with a little bow that managed to be both gracious and deserving, made them move over so she could put her granddaughter down. The child lay flat on her back on the treacherously cavernous couch, her bright red jacket and pants overlapping so thickly that her tummy rose up high – with a floppy knitted button right on top. Lying there fast asleep, she looked like a little red mountain.

'Ah – so now she's asleep!' Mrs Tong started to unbutton her long gown so she could cover her grandchild, but Mrs Bao, who knew her from these visits to the clinic, stopped her. 'Here – use my rain cape to cover the child.' Mrs Tong thanked Mrs Bao, then eased into a rocking chair and started chatting with her. Mrs Bao was quite ugly; she had a long, winter-melon face and strangely ringed, cartoon-like eyes, with a fleshy, drooping nose. Because she'd never been good-looking, she'd always been consigned to the role of female companion, forever sympathizing with others. Feeling Mrs Bao's warmth, Mrs Tong started in, right away, on her sorrows.

'I'm just waiting till Mr Pang here gets me back on my feet, and the military situation settles down, and my three girls are all married – then I'm headed off to a convent somewhere. It's all this aggravation that's doing me in – my legs can barely hold me up, I'm so sick with aggravation. Every day I cook for them, and when I go and wash up . . .' She toyed with the gold band on her finger, tugging it back and forth. 'While I'm washing up, there they are, the whole lot of them – my old man, his concubine, his sister – sitting around the table, polishing off all the best dishes before I even get there.

'My husband got himself into trouble, and when they hauled him off to district headquarters, I was scared half to death. I got him out of there all right, with my god-daughter's help, and seven thousand dollars. Oh, it was awful! Riding in a pedicab at night – bumpity-thump, bumpity-thump – you know those cobblestone streets in Suzhou, so narrow and hard to find. It's a wonder I didn't fall out and break my neck, there in the dark! Finally, I got him out. And wouldn't you think that I'd want to know what it was like in there, and he'd want to know how I got him out? But no – he disappeared the minute we got home – into the concubine's room!'

Everyone burst out laughing. Mrs Bao wrinkled up her brow and laughed; Mrs Tong laughed too, her eyes reddening.

She clapped her hands together, and spittle flew from her mouth.

'Of course I was angry, so angry I couldn't sleep. The next morning I said to him, right out – here I was so horribly worried, and you didn't even tell me what it was like in there, didn't even ask me how I got you out. And you know what he said? He said, "Who asked you to get me out? Throwing away money like that, when I was perfectly fine in there." "Oh my goodness," I said, "so you were fine and dandy – if I hadn't gotten my god-daughter to help out, and put a phone call through, you wouldn't have been put in the cashier's room – where you were so fine and dandy! If you'd been put in a real gaol cell, do you think you'd have been so very comfy?" So, Mrs Bao, you see why I'm so angry – if it weren't for those three girls of mine, I'd never have borne it this long.'

'Well, but your children are all grown now,' Mrs Bao reminded her. 'As long as they remember their duty, you'll be fine.'

'My children are all good to me, and so are my daughters-in-law. They're proper young women from good, old-fashioned homes – I picked them out myself. Oh, Mrs Bao – even though I say I'm leaving them all, it's not an easy thing to do! Of course, I could go to the head of the clan, but he's from a branch that's junior to ours, so telling him would be too embarrassing.'

Mrs Bao chuckled. 'Well, look – you shouldn't leave your family, not at your age. You've got good years ahead.'

Mrs Tong sighed. 'So that's why I always tell my daughters not to get married. There's nothing to be gained from it. Here I am, the only one who worries about money – he never so much as raises a hair over it.'

Mrs Xi spoke up admiringly. 'You're a female head of household, that's what you are, Mrs Tong.'

Mrs Tong pounded her fist into her palm, then opened both hands wide and held them out. 'It's been thirty years since I came into his family, and in that time I've done everything for them. Back when I was first married, I got up every day in the dark, fetched the water for his parents' morning face-wash, soft-boiled their eggs, did everything just right. Then I had children, lots of them, and that means lots of work of course. My attitude towards his parents was very, uh . . . they always said I was a good daughter-in-law, they did.' Here she suddenly fell silent. Those old folks, the ones who'd been so hard on her, and whom she had finally vanquished, they were now long dead; and still she rose every morning before dawn, rustling about in rooms that were like the inside of a dark red bucket: scritchy-scratch, running her hands over long-familiar surfaces, everything the same, except for the sharp, cold ache in her knuckles.

'Don't be angry, Mrs Tong,' Mrs Xi chided her. 'Don't know if you've tried this before – just go and listen to one of those Christian ministers, not that you have to believe it all. I know some ladies who suffered from aggravation, and they went and listened to the ministers' talk. Now they're not angry any more, they're nice and fat.'

It was Mrs Bao's turn for a massage, and the room fell silent for a while. Mrs Tong sat with her hands folded, a solid chunk of rightful misery. Her eyes were red, her lips muttered and sputtered, the way old people do when they're lonely and cold. Black-and-white kitchen tiles rose under her feet, and everything around her felt as if it had been wiped with a damp kitchen cloth. In the inner room, a wall-clock ticked away, counting minutes and seconds with punctilious care, cutting time into tiny little squares for the civilized world. But far in the distance one could hear the noontime cockcrow, just a faint note or two, as if the land stretched out, uninhabited, for miles and miles.

Mrs Bao came out and took back her rain cape. Mrs Tong again started to unbutton her long grey outer gown, so she could cover her granddaughter.

'Oh, but then you'll be cold,' said Mrs Xi.

'No, no, not at all.'

'Use my coat instead.' Mrs Xi took off her light green coat. Mrs Tong thanked her, and the two of them started chatting again.

'Don't be angry,' said Mrs Xi. 'You should just keep to your own room, and ignore them. Things have gotten really bad, or haven't you heard? Up in the interior they've issued a new order: since too many Chinese have died in the war, the men can marry again, and they aren't even called concubines – they're second wives! They're telling the men to take another wife!'

Mrs Tong could barely hear her, she was in such a daze – her fortune-favoured fat face suddenly went all scarred and scabrous, pink and numb. 'Huh? huh? . . . It's really bad these days, isn't it? A fortune-teller once told me that I'm the Womb of the Earth Bodhisattva come to life again, my husband's the Dog Star – we're vengeful lovers locked in mortal combat, no good end in sight. A lot of fortune-tellers have told me this, actually.'

'Mrs Tong, you should go to a Christian church some time. Listen to them for a while, and then you won't feel so upset any more. Any church will do. There's one just down the way from here, in fact.'

Mrs Tong nodded, then asked: 'In Suzhou, at the Golden Light Temple, there's a monk called the All-Around Enlightened One – have you heard of him?'

Mrs Xi nodded. Then, suddenly remembering something else, she leaned over close and asked, keeping her voice low: 'Do you know any remedies for hair that's falling out? Look here, at my hair – see, the hairline's way back here!'

Mrs Tong answered with well-practised ease. 'Take some ginger slices and rub them on your scalp – that's strong medicine, that is.'

Mrs Xi had a well-trained, scientific mind. 'How often should I rub my scalp with the ginger?'

'How often? Oh, whenever you think of it. And let me tell you – that monk at the Golden Light Temple, *he*'s strong medicine. He asked me, "Do you scrap a lot, you and your husband?" I said we did. "You must stop that right away," he said. "You've got lots of grievances from previous lives, and if you don't fix up things with him this time, you'll just come back as husband and wife, and things will be worse for you. He won't let you off so easy, next time round – he'll make a beggar of you!" I held my hands together, and I said, "Thank you, Master. I will take your words home with me!" And from that day on I really did it, I never raised my voice no matter how angry I was. Before, I had such a grip on him that he thought I was one of the emperor's trained assassins, swooping in with magical powers – he was that afraid of me. But after he stopped being afraid of me, he ran around to sing-song girls, and even brought women home with him. Now he's worse than ever before – all because I let up on him way too soon!' She heaved a sigh.

Mrs Xi had by now lost all patience. During this long recital, she'd started out with murmurs of assent, and little nods of the head, which soon enough gave way to mere eyelash-dips, as her little mouth pursed out like a bird's beak, full of opinions looking for a chance to break out, till further consideration made her decide not to waste her breath on a hoary old fool like Mrs Tong.

It was now the little boy's turn, the boy who'd been brought by a maid, and he was screaming and crying. 'Don't cry,' Mr Pang kept saying to him, 'the doctor likes you!'

The maid cajoled and fawned all at the same time: 'The doctor likes you! There, there now – the doctor likes you! When you grow up and get married, you'll have to invite him to your wedding!'

'Oh, yes!' said Mr Pang, smiling. 'Some day, when the situation in Shanghai settles down and you get married, you'd better invite me or I'll be angry, that's for sure!'

Mrs Tong asked for the time, got very worried about it, and paid an extra two hundred to skip ahead of the others. When she was finished, she picked up her soundly sleeping granddaughter, gave Mrs Xi's coat back to her, thanked Mrs Xi again, and had no idea that anyone was feeling less than cordial towards her.

Mrs Tong stood there in her underclothing, a lightly padded black linen jacket with matching pants. Her short, pot-bellied figure and full face, daubed with red and white makeup, made her look like an old-time Chinese boy, like the ones in those paintings on the theme 'A Hundred Sons'. She took her grey wool outer gown off the hook and slowly put it on. She twirled it through the air, and for a moment the entire room was wrapped up in it. The grown swirled across the face and shoulders of Mrs Xi, who ducked in disgust. Mrs Tong did up the buttons, except for those at the throat. Feeling that she needed to explain, she smiled at Mrs Xi as she went out with the child in her arms, and said: 'Might have to cover her up again outside – don't want her to catch cold when she wakes up.' Then she said goodbye.

A new client had come in, and paid extra to jump the line.

Mrs Xi stood at the door of the treatment room and looked in, then sadly went back to her seat.

The client seemed to be a young man of the gentry class. He had a deerskin overcoat and talked with Mr Pang about the war documentary that was being shown at the Russian Club. 'It's really frightful. You see the shrapnel flying by, and a soldier falls backward, his face twisted up in pain, and then he clutches at his chest and dies. And so many, many!'

Mr Pang stared and nodded. 'What savagery! When you fight a war you really do kill people – it's not like massage, the way I make people squeal with pain, but I'm doing it for their own good!' He chuckled, then sighed.

'So many dead – mountains of them,' the young man said.

Mr Pang sighed, feeling a touch of sympathy. 'Well, our war here is nothing, if you compare it with that war over there! Too savage for words. Where did you say you saw the film?'

'At the Russian Club.'

'They really have this kind of film there? How much does it cost to get in?'

'I can pick up tickets for you, if you like.'

There was a long pause, and then Mr Pang asked, 'What time is the show? Is it every day?'

'It's at eight o'clock. How many tickets do you want?'

Another long pause. 'It had better be good,' he said at last, with a smile.

Mrs Pang cut in from the other room: 'It had better show lots of *other* people dying –' Then she started to guffaw. Mr Pang laughed right along with his wife.

The clinic window was closed, and the window-panes covered with criss-cross strips of yellowing newspaper that had been pasted up in case of air attack, and were now peeling off.

It was a pure white, overcast day, as if the window had been pasted over with cellophane.

Mrs Pang smiled as she went over to open the window. She looked up and down the street, aimlessly, then sniffed a few times and tossed out a used toothpick. She rinsed her mouth with tea from the half-empty cup that sat on the table, then spat into the dark mouth of the white ceramic spittoon. The spittoon was next to Mrs Xi's feet. Mrs Xi smiled, but Mrs Pang pretended not to see her; those laughing, lamp-like eyes of hers were like lights on the second floor of a house, ignoring everyone below. Mrs Xi felt it, and looked away. But the gold-rimmed mirror on the wall showed Mrs Pang pursing up her lips: a dark, wizened face with the mouth scrunched up tight, twitching impatiently. Mrs Xi quickly looked out the window again. She felt hurt, a bit abused, and so thought softly of her husband. 'He'll come back, and when he does . . . once he sees me, he'll feel bad about what he's done. All I have to do is be nice to him . . .'

Consoling herself with these thoughts, she picked up the paper and started to read it, her mouth pointed out sharply like a feeding bird's, pulled over to one side a bit, full of reservations and disapproval. Her husband would come back some day. Not too late – please don't let it be too late! But not too early either. That hair of hers needed time to grow back.

It was a filmy, white-dark day. The brownish-green leaves of a plane tree were just outside the window; they were as big as a hand, and almost transparent. Across the street there was a row of old, red-brick houses, and even though it was a cloudy day, the balconies were strung with long, neat lines of laundry. A cat walked across the roof, black like a cloud shadow on snow – the only parts that showed were his black back and snake-like tail, gently waving in the air. A moment later, he reappeared on the balcony, slowly walking along the top of the railing; looking neither left nor right, the cat just kept going on.

And life kept going on, walking its own way.

*Translated by Karen S. Kingsbury*

# GREAT FELICITY

The two Lou sisters, one named Erqiao, the other, Simei, went for a fitting at the Xiangyun Clothing Emporium. It was their brother's wedding in two days and they were going to be bridesmaids. Erqiao asked the clerk, 'Is the bride here already?' 'Yes, she is. She's in the fitting room inside.' Simei tugged at Erqiao, 'Look at that piece of yellow fabric hanging there, the one with the bias stripes.' Erqiao said, 'You already have a yellow dress.' Simei smiled, 'Why not get a couple more while you can? Father can't very well get upset with anyone just now.' They went over to feel the fabric; they asked how much it was, and whether the colour would run.

Erqiao took a look at her shoes. 'I shouldn't have worn these shoes today. They're the wrong height for trying on the dresses.' 'What shoes are you going to wear on the day?' Simei asked. 'Same as yours. Yuqing will be wearing flat shoes. She's taller than our brother – mustn't make him look too short, must she?' Simei said in a low voice, 'Yuqing's figure . . . brother hasn't seen what she looks like when she takes off her clothes . . .'

The two of them burst into giggles. Erqiao looked around them, 'Shh! Shh!' Then Simei said, 'She is so stiff you could say "when thrown to the ground there arises the music of bronze bells and stone drums"!' Erqiao laughed. 'Where did you get that? Aren't you poetic! But really, we wouldn't have known what she really looks like if we hadn't been trying on clothes together. Our poor brother . . . for the rest of his life . . .' Simei doubled up with laughter. 'The slightest touch and you can hear her bones knocking together. It is probably all right dancing with her, because the music would drown it out. It's a bit strange really. It's not that she's at all thin, so why is she all bones?'

Erqiao said, 'Big frame.'

'Her skin is white enough, it's just a pity she reminds you the other way of the White Bone Demon!' Erqiao laughed and gave her a slap. 'It's not *that* bad. Ah, poor brother. No use telling him now. It's too late . . .'

Simei said, 'I think she must be at least thirty.'

'Brother is twenty-six; she's saying that she's twenty-six too.'

'It wouldn't be hard to find out. She has so many younger brothers and sisters. If she faked her age, then the younger ones would have to fake theirs too. It's easy to tell from the little ones.'

Erqiao gestured. 'They are all stacked up like dominoes. If you push the first one back in years, they will all fall backwards with a clatter!' They laughed hysterically. Then Erqiao said, 'The littlest one has just been born. You can't make him fall back into the womb, can you?'

Simei laughed. 'I'll ask Tangqian in school tomorrow. She's Yuqing's cousin, you know.'

'You know Tangqian and Liqian well then?'

'They have been quite friendly to me lately.'

Erqiao wagged a cautioning finger at Simei. 'Watch out. After big brother marries Yuqing, there's still another brother left at home. I'm afraid they all have their eyes on him too. Can't blame them for being envious. Yuqing is just no match for our brother – and I'm not the only one who thinks so. Her relatives are even more unspeakable. Each one poorer than the last.'

Yuqing stood with her back to the mirror, looking over her shoulder for a back view. She was not as ungainly as her sisters-in-law made her out to be. At least, not in the silvery-white, long-sleeved wedding gown. Thus formally attired, she was very presentable – what the newspaper ads might call a lady of refinement. In comparison, Erqiao and Simei were simply young ladies of the *nouveau riche*. Although their father had scholarly pretensions, he'd only made his fortune in recent years, and the daughters still had this air of fresh and vulgar merriment.

They said hello to Yuqing, then shooed the shop assistant out and started changing, struggling to pull their dresses over their heads. Through their slips one could see their petulant, pouting breasts.

Yuqing gave her dress a tug and asked, 'Do you think this needs altering?' Erqiao gave her a dutiful glance, then said, 'Looks fine!' Yuqing was still worrying that it might be a little too long in the back, when Simei suddenly gave a squeal. She had discovered that the gauze top and the georgette bottom of her gown were two different shades of pink. Each of them felt that hers was the most important role in the wedding. For Erqiao and Simei, Yuqing was the dazzling white caption to appear on the silver screen at the end of a movie – 'The End', while they were the exciting previews for the 'Next Change'.

When the clerk came in, Erqiao and Simei both started to complain. The clerk was eager to please, offering to raise it a bit here, tuck it in a bit there. 'There is no mistake. The measurements are all here: waist, nineteen inches; shoulders: fourteen and a half and fourteen for her. No mistake there.

Colours not right? That can be changed – no problem, no problem. Let's do this: we'll bleach the top a bit; we have a special solution for that. If that's not enough, we'll re-dye the skirt. No problem, no problem.' The clerk was a young fellow of fifteen or sixteen, dressed in a mandarin gown of grey cotton. His smooth white face wore a permanent slick smile. He was extremely patient. Listening to him, one would never have guessed that the evening gowns were only being hired out to these two women. As spiritual and as graceful as a tall narcissus, it was hard to imagine how far he might go when he grew up.

The décor of the Xiangyun Emporium was in something called 'palace style', its red walls complete with gold dragon reliefs. The walls of the fitting room were hung with full-length mirrors and there were bridal pictures everywhere – different heads with different smiles sticking out of the same hired bridal gown. There was a kind of egalitarian and inhuman cheer about the little vermilion room. Yuqing pushed away the jumble of gowns on the aquamarine china stool and sat down. She leaned slightly forward, chin in hand, and watched her two bridesmaids moodily. Yuqing was very careful not to let her excitement show – to be beside yourself with delight at getting married was a sure sign of an eager spinster. Yuqing's face was smooth and blank, like a freshly made bed; with the heavy imprint of sadness upon it now, it looked as if someone had plonked themselves down on the bed.

Erqiao asked Yuqing, 'Are you almost done shopping?'

Yuqing frowned, 'Not nearly! I've been running around all morning. It's so hard to shop these days. Things that are even passable are too expensive. But you can't not buy them either, because they will just be more expensive later.' Erqiao put out a hand. 'Let me see the dress fabric you bought.' Yuqing handed

her a package. 'It's a silk-linen blend.' Erqiao poked a hole in
the wrapping-paper and brought the package up to her face, as
if to suck the contents out through the hole like a mosquito
sucking the yolk out of an egg through the shell. She said,
'Pattern's not bad.' Simei said, 'It was quite popular for a while
last year.' Erqiao said, 'But I'm afraid it will fade. I had something
like that. It got all washed out.' Yuqing blushed and snatched
the package back, saying, 'The difference is in the quality. They
have a cheaper version of the same pattern. But I am the type
who won't buy anything that won't last.'

Yuqing had also bought a satin embroidered nightdress, a
matching embroidered robe, a silk padded morning gown,
embroidered padded slippers, a *cloisonné* compact and a purse
mirror with its own zippered suede cover. She believed that a
woman only had one chance in her life to indulge herself, and
she should make the most of it. Whatever she saw, she bought,
as if there was no tomorrow. There was a kind of valediction
and desolation in her heart. Her sadness as she shopped for her
trousseau was not entirely put on.

Watching her spend money, her in-laws thought her too
extravagant. Even though it was her own money she was
spending, it still infuriated the two sisters-in-law. Yuqing's was
an eminent family in decline. Her parents had scraped together
50,000 for her dowry and now she was spending it all on herself.
Erqiao, Simei and Sanduo, the brother-in-law, gossiping behind
her back, had learned that according to old Chinese customs,
everything in the newly-weds' room, except for the bed, was to
be furnished by the bride's side. The Western custom was
different; but there, on top of having to bring a sum of money
as her dowry, the woman also had to provide all the linen for
the new household. Whichever custom she went by, Yuqing
was wrong to be so irresponsible. The parents-in-law had come

off badly in the deal, but suffered in silence. However, the sisters-in-law, also indirectly affected, were less inclined to be good-natured about it.

After Erqiao and Simei had inspected Yuqing's purchases, they felt personally cheated. Even when they tried to look at it objectively, from the outside, they still couldn't help feeling that it was a shame the stupid woman spent her money in such bad taste.

Of course, they kept smiling. Erqiao smiled and asked, 'Do you have shoes to go with the rose-coloured gown you're wearing after the ceremony?' Yuqing said, 'Didn't I tell you? What a bother! That colour is impossible to match. I've been to so many shoe stores. Embroidered shoes only come in bright red, pink or burgundy.' Simei said, 'Don't bother to look any more. My ma heard that you couldn't find any shoes, so she's making you a pair.' Yuqing said, 'Oh, that's really too . . . anyway, there's no time.' Simei said, 'That's Ma for you. There are so many other more urgent things waiting to be taken care of, and there she is making shoes! There's so much to do at home just now.' Erqiao was embarrassed – her mother always embarrassed her. But she couldn't really not defend her in front of others. So she said, 'We have a seamstress at home and she could easily have asked her to rush a pair out. But Ma's like that – even if she might not make a good job of it, she feels that this is a way of expressing her affection.' Yuqing felt that she should be touched and was a little uncomfortable. She said, 'That's really too . . . really too . . .' over and over, then she changed her clothes quickly and left the store alone, dragging her head of weary hair to the hairdresser's. Her permed hair felt the heaviness of the rainy day. Please don't let it rain the day after tomorrow.

Mrs Lou was only too happy to make the shoes for her new

daughter-in-law, because she felt that she was not up to the
tasks before her – despite all the practice she'd had over the last
twenty to thirty years. Tracing and cutting patterns for shoes
had been her daily tasks before she got married and she was
thrilled to have an excuse to retreat into her girlhood memories.
Actually, she couldn't even sew very well, but no one really
valued or paid attention to such things any more. No one would
notice that the stitches were too big or too far apart, or that the
toecaps were crooked: things which would have made her
sisters and friends laugh at her in the old days.

Though she frowned over the work and tried to look as if
she felt put upon, the whole family seemed able to see through
her. They knew that the shoes brought her some kind of
enjoyment and they all begrudged her it.

Her husband, Lou Xiaobo, came back very late from his
office at the bank as usual. Once home, he was impatient for
the maid to draw his bath. He put on his slippers and lay on the
couch to rest while he flipped through an old *Esquire* magazine.
The Americans really knew how to advertise their products.
Above every car floated a little fluff of cuddly white cloud.
'Four Roses' whiskey had crystal-clear yellow liquor in a crystal-
clear glass on a glossy brown table. Beside it lay some red roses
– such elegance just for a glass of liquor. Xiaobo reached for his
cup of tea on the round table next to the couch and his eye fell
on the rose-coloured embroidered upper of a slipper being
pressed under the glass top of the table. The flat gold flowers
glittered in the light. He suddenly felt as if his learning and his
wealth had come together in a kind of tasteful sophistication,
that his scholarly ambitions were now satisfied. Xiaobo had a
degree from America, he was a real scholar. However, his later
fulfilment in life had nothing to do with his long period as a
student.

The other rose-coloured shoe upper was still in Mrs Lou's hands. When Xiaobo saw it, he couldn't help saying, 'Must you do that in the midst of everything? Can't you put it aside?' Looking at his wife, he could have gone on and on: 'Do you *have* to cut your hair in a duck tail? If it's convenience you're after, just shave your head. Do you *have* to wear lilac stockings? And do you *have* to roll them down below your knees? Do you *have* to let your black slip show through the slit of your cheongsam?' His voice would be strained with impatience, yet he would adopt a conciliatory tone, for he had a reputation for being a good husband. Who else would have found someone like Mrs Lou through a matchmaker, and come back from his studies abroad to have four children with her, and stick with her for thirty years?

Mrs Lou wore eyeglasses. When she frowned, her eyebrows formed an upside-down 'V'. Her face was like a dumpling made by a child playing with dough that had been pinched and kneaded till the dirt from the hands got into the flour, making it a sort of dirty white.

Lou Xiaobo also wore glasses and had a plump, round face, but he was his wife's exact opposite – a most capable man, especially good at managing people in social situations. He was a tall man, and though he wore Western suits, he made people think of a graceful dancer with flowing sleeves. His social skills were, in truth, a kind of dance that dazzled his audience and made their heads spin while he twirled *en pointe*.

Mr and Mrs Lou were such a mismatched couple that many people felt indignant on his behalf. Mrs Lou knew this very well and it angered her. Though she often let him have his way in private, she deliberately insulted her husband in front of others, just to show them how Mr Lou both loved and feared her, that things were not as outsiders might think.

Because there were two maids in the room preparing for the wedding, Mrs Lou could not let what Mr Lou had said to her go. She immediately scowled and said, 'What does my making shoes have to do with you? Busybody!'

Xiaobo said nothing more. Usually, he let her have her way in front of other people. If she wanted other people to think of her as bad-tempered and sour, that was up to her. He had already sacrificed this much, he might as well be the good husband to the end. However, he was a bit impatient today. The scenes of glossy luxury in the magazine ads and the wealth that he saw in front of his own eyes did not seem to tally. One belonged in the magazine; the other in his own home. He silently said to his wife, 'Why must you make yourself look stupid?' Impatient, but still conciliatory. When the maid told him his bath was ready, he stood up and let his magazine fall to the floor. He didn't bother to pick it up.

Mrs Lou realized that Xiaobo was annoyed. It was all because she wanted to save face when there were people around. She had always resented the people around her. It wasn't as if she didn't realize that if the people who cared about her were all to die, leaving her and her husband to rattle around in the empty house alone, her husband would not bother about her at all. Why be a responsible husband when there's no one to see? She knew that she should really be grateful to the people around her, so she hated them even more.

The clock struck nine. Erqiao and Simei came home by bicycle. They had first gone to their brother and sister-in-law's new home to help decorate and to deliver gifts from friends and relatives. They brought back two baskets woven of handkerchiefs which they had taken there earlier. Yuqing had disliked the design of the handkerchiefs, and she thought such baskets were too vulgar anyway. Their home was too small and there was nowhere these baskets could be kept out of sight. Just as the girls were explaining, two more baskets were delivered. Mrs Lou and her two daughters tipped the delivery boy in some confusion. Mrs Lou still couldn't bear to put down the embroidered shoe upper. It was dangling from a piece of cotton threaded through a needle on her bosom. The sight of the shoe jogged Simei's memory: 'Ma, forget those shoes. Yuqing found a pair.'

Mrs Lou didn't quite hear the undertone of vindictive pleasure in her daughter's casual remarks. Mrs Lou also pretended not to mind at all. 'Ah, she found a pair, did she?' So saying, she pulled the thread from the needle and pressed the unfinished shoe upper under the glass table-top.

Then they discovered that an acquaintance they had not invited to the wedding had sent a gift, so an invitation had to be sent to him. Mrs Lou asked the maid to find out if the young master was home. When the maid reported that he was, Mrs Lou asked him to write out the invitation. Dalu was a head shorter than his father, with a placid, small face and ears that stuck out, like Bashful in *Snow White*. But in fact he was a garrulous sort and started giving an account of expenses incurred immediately he came in. He was surprised at how much it cost to set up a small household. He had rented two rooms in a friend's house. The floors had to be waxed and the bathtub scoured, and the west-facing windows needed bamboo blinds. Besides regular curtains, they also needed black-out blinds and the colours mustn't clash with the rug and the chairs. Lamps needed shades and bulbs. For mahjong, an extra table was needed with its own tablecloth and lamp – Yuqing knew all about such things. There were two rooms plus the kitchen and, if they were going to live a life of probity and seriousness, each room must have a clock in it. Dalu spent his parents' money with a clear conscience, because he was not marrying just anyone. The best thing about Yuqing was that she had breeding. She brought out the best in everyone. Take his father for example – whenever he saw Yuqing, he would start talking politics. He would hold forth continuously for a couple of hours, then he would turn to the company and praise Yuqing for being such an unusually knowledgeable woman.

The young couple were both knowledgeable people. In shopping for their new home they had bought the little things first, leaving the important things till last, so that when they had used up their money they could ask for more – a bed, for example, was a must. Mrs Lou exclaimed, 'You kids have no planning!' She loved her son, but she loved her money, too. She felt a gentle tug at her heart-strings. 'I'll give you my bed. I'll just use your single one.' Erqiao, Sanduo and Simei protested with one voice: 'That's no good. There will be many guests here over the next couple of days. There has always been a set of two double beds in Ma's room. If all of a sudden one is gone, replaced by a single bed, people will say that the daughter-in-law came in and broke the household up. You can't do that. With Father, reputation comes first.'

While they were talking, Xiaobo came out, bathrobe over his shoulders, and pointed at Mrs Lou with his glasses, which were all steamed up. 'That's so typical of all of you. Leaving everything until the last possible minute. When I saw that suite of teak furniture at the auction house last year, I wanted to buy it for Dalu. You wouldn't listen to me then.' Dalu laughed, 'I hadn't even met Yuqing then.' Xiaobo glared at him, then, feeling that his look wasn't impressive enough, put on his glasses and glared at him again. Mrs Lou was afraid father and son might get into a row and quickly said, 'Really, it's a pity we didn't buy it at the time. Since Dalu would have gotten married sooner or later, we couldn't have gone wrong with it.'

Xiaobo stuck out his chin, 'Do I have to take care of every-thing in this household? What have you been doing? Whenever the children were absent from school, I had to be the one to write their excuses.' These two things weren't really related, but Mrs Lou knew that Xiaobo had more than once made the same kind of complaint in front of the relatives. Though she felt that her husband was justified, she had her own grievances and felt deprived of an outlet. Suddenly it all welled up within her and she wanted to answer back: 'If we have been treating you badly here at home, then don't come back! I'm sure you have another woman outside. That's why you keep finding fault with things at home – this won't do, that won't do.' Then she remembered that she was going to be a mother-in-law soon and swallowed her words. She put her shoulders back and clattered to the bathroom where she gargled noisily, swishing the water around in her mouth, then spitting it out with a vengeance. Whenever Mrs Lou was angry and wanted to cry, she always channelled her impulse into bluff and hearty action – letting it all out.

Outside the bathroom, father and son continued talking. Xiaobo had asked, with a slightly challenging tone in his voice, 'Who was it that sent the gift that came just now? Anyone I know?' Dalu said, 'A man from our company.' Xiaobo was surprised. 'Everybody from the office pitched in for a joint gift. Why does he have to give you a separate one? Do we have to give him an invitation? Is he one of your drinking buddies?' Dalu explained, 'He is from the accounts department. He is one of Mr Feng's men.' Xiaobo understood immediately and changed his whole tone of voice, switching the topic of Mr Feng and how the tabloids had been making a joke of him.

They were, after all, father and son. Mrs Lou felt isolated. The whole Lou family, her husband, her children, the young and old, so handsome, so competitive, she loved them all and they, time after time, banded together to think of different ways to prove her inadequate. Her husband had always been concerned about his reputation even when they were poor. He had always loved to socialize and was therefore always putting her in various embarrassing situations and, time and again, finding that she didn't measure up. As the family became wealthy, it should have meant an easier time, but she hadn't realized that as the parties became grander, she would find herself even more inadequate.

However, if you told her to live differently, to forgo the nice clothes, the visits and return visits, she would be unhappy then too and feel bereft. Prosperity, frustration, embarrassment – this was life. Mrs Lou felt another tug at her heartstrings. As she stood at the washbasin, facing the mirror, she felt an itch, as if something had fallen under the rim of her glasses. She thought it was a teardrop. With a corner of her handkerchief around a finger, she rubbed it and found that it was just a little green bug attracted by the light. Mrs Lou took off her glasses and looked and looked again, pulling up the lid to inspect her eye, afraid a bug might have got inside. She stood right up close to the mirror, almost pressing her face to it. She gazed at herself, at her pale, stolid, spreading cheeks – she couldn't even articulate to herself her own misery. The eyebrows were drawn together, always frowning, but her expression said only, 'Oh bother! Bother!' and nothing of her misery.

Although the couple had had a tiff, the next day, when

something came up, his wife still called Xiaobo at the office to ask his advice. The retired director of transport was supposed to serve as chief witness for the marriage ceremony. But though he was no longer an official, like all officials, he covered his tracks well. He had slipped out of Shanghai without so much as a by-your-leave. Xiaobo couldn't come up with anyone comparable at a moment's notice, so he asked his wife to look up a man named Li, who was the director of a hospital, and had a certain cachet as well. Mrs Lou went by car to his house, braving the rain. Once inside the Li house, she opened her wet umbrella and set it on the sitting-room carpet. She took off her sky-blue transparent rain cape, held it by the collar and shook the water from it. Then she took out a handkerchief to wipe the drops from her leather overcoat. The leather coat hadn't been buttoned up and fell open all the way down to reveal her splayed feet. Rain cape in hand, she looked around, then put the dripping cape on the sofa and sat down herself. Dr Li was not at home. Mrs Li came out to greet her. Mrs Lou gave her a business card with 'Lou Xiaobo' on it and said, 'Xiaobo and Dr Li are well acquainted.' Mrs Li was Cantonese and could only manage a few stilted phrases of Mandarin. She didn't seem very clear about anything. Fortunately, Mrs Lou had absolute confidence in Xiaobo's reputation and was therefore able to state the purpose of her visit with composure. Mrs Li said, 'I will let him know and have him call you.' Mrs Lou then handed over two canisters of tea, which Mrs Li did her best to refuse. Mrs Lou was determined that she should have them, but when Mrs Li finally accepted, her manner had taken on a definite chill. Mrs Lou felt that she had made a mess of things once again. However, with thirty years of countless *faux pas* behind her, she sat on, impervious. She sat until it was time to go, then she stood up, put on her rain cape and took her leave. It wasn't till she got to the door that she discovered that she had left her umbrella inside and turning back to retrieve it, nodded at Mrs Li again – a reserved nod indicating that the other's status was too humble for a bow.

The truth was, Mrs Lou did feel nervous about the whole visit. She opened her umbrella even before she got out of the door, then discovered that she couldn't pass through and had to close the umbrella, once again splattering the floor with rainwater.

Dr Li called later to say that he would officiate at the wedding.

It was still raining the day of the wedding. The Lous were worried that too few guests would show up. Their fears were groundless, however. In these times, who would give a gift and not come to eat his share? The ceremony was at three in the afternoon. By two-thirty, the hall was already filling up, with the guests naturally divided into two groups. The groom's guests sat on one side; the bride's on the other. Everybody was smiling, chatting, fluttering back and forth, some pulling down seats to sit on. In the grand hall, there were great red pillars entwined with green dragons. The walls were of black glass and a black glass altar held a little gold Buddha. This was the Orient as a little old foreign lady might imagine it. Under all stretched a vast floral Peking carpet. You walked on the carpet, but your feet never touched the flowers woven into it – there was always something in between. The huge room with its colourful decorations was like a big glass globe, with shifting patterns of colour at its centre. The guests were all flies climbing gingerly over the surface of the globe, trying to get inside.

There were two who, not content with lingering awhile, fretted their limbs outside the glass ball, and plotted how to get into the luxurious interior. Yuqing's five girl cousins had all come with their mother. The eldest and the second were nice enough girls, but they were not young any more and were getting over-anxious. The second, Liqian, had had an unlined cheongsam specially made for the occasion. However, she was not prepared for the unexpected drop in temperature after two days of rain. It was too early for the hotel to turn the heating on so she was unable to take off her old overcoat, not because she couldn't bear the cold, but because she couldn't stand the concerned queries, 'Aren't you cold?' Liqian was born unlucky. Although she got there early, somehow she could not find a seat. She was leaning against a pillar – she liked to do things like that. Her pale exhausted face was a challenge; it seemed to say, 'I am tired of this world. That's why I am also tired of you – are you tired of me?' The challenge lay in the unexpected twist at the end.

Her sister, Tangqian, was not as tall as her, but her face was fuller, so at first glance she looked younger. Tangqian was a spirited girl. But in spite of all her years of spiritedness, she was still unmarried, and she was beginning to lose her self-confidence. Her little round soul had shattered, and had been repaired with white china. Her eyes were white china, so were her teeth, which were slightly protruding – hard, white as snow and every bit as cold and cruel. But she kept smiling and was even more spirited. Seeing one of her cousins from afar, she immediately stood up to beckon her to come sit by her, and gave up her chair for her. She sat on the armrest instead, pointing and gesturing, chatting and laughing. More quietly she asked if the usher standing at the door was the groom's brother. When she heard that he was only a clerk from Xiaobo's bank, she lost interest. More and more relatives were arriving. She greeted and chatted with each one, holding their hands warmly. Tangqian's laughing voice seemed to have teeth. At first, the teeth nibbled and teased, but eventually, their bite became painful.

The band struck up. The magnificent procession of bride, groom, groomsmen and bridesmaids marched slowly in. In that moment of breathless anticipation, there was goodwill and poetry: pink and pale yellow bridesmaids were like the colourful clouds of dawn. The black-jacketed men were like swallows, dark shadows gliding through the clouds. The white bride with her half-closed eyes was like a corpse who had not quite awakened at the dawn of its resurrection – her glow was understated. All were ushered in to the strains of uplifting music.

When the bride and groom came to a stop, the chief witness made his speech: 'Ladies and gentlemen. I . . . today . . . am very . . . happy . . .' The atmosphere immediately changed. The chief witness mentioned the new morality, new thinking and the responsibilities of citizens. He hoped that the couple would be diligent in producing little citizens. Everybody laughed. Then it was a speech from the person who had introduced the couple to each other. He didn't have to stand on ceremony and could be as creative as he wanted. His main point: this man and woman will be sleeping together in a little while. Take a good look at them now, because a little later, you won't be able to. The speaker's difficulty was that he was not allowed to say any of this directly, but fortunately his audience understood him and knew to laugh. But the speech dragged on too long and hardly anyone was laughing by the end.

The band struck up the recessional. As the bride left, her white wedding gown seemed a little worn, her face likewise.

The guests started cheering and showering them with confetti. The people at the back threw confetti all over the people in front. Tangqian had been staring at the best man, the groom's brother, Sanduo, throughout the ceremony. Suddenly, she let out a wild hoot of joy and threw a whole bag of confetti at him.

The bride, the groom and the attendants went to have their pictures taken. The guests went next door for tea. Tangqian, spiritedly, and Liqian, coolly, ate their cake.

Halfway through, the bride and groom came back. The band started up again. The bride and groom were the first on to the dance floor. This was the young people's arena. Even those who didn't dance crowded around the dance floor to watch. The older ladies stood quietly at the back, smiling discreetly. Even though they had been pushed out of the limelight, they retained a sort of negative importance, like a seal squarely stamped on a painting. Without it, the painting is valueless.

Nobody invited Tangqian to dance. She kept smiling, as if she had a slab of white china in her mouth, and couldn't close it up.

Tangqian and Liqian were wondering if they should leave early, before people began to disperse, in order to make an impression, to give people the chance to inquire who the beautiful woman in blue was. Just as they were getting ready to leave, a woman they knew well came over to their table, and started complaining to their mother. 'Isn't there anyone in charge here? We don't have anything at our table. There really should be someone in charge of each table.' Their mother immediately served her some tea. She sat down and proceeded to shove food into her mouth, neither eagerly nor coldly, just totally impassively. As there was no way Tangqian and Liqian could express their disgust, they could only urge their mother to leave.

When they spotted Sanduo standing beside Mrs Lou, they went up to them to say goodbye. Mrs Lou was confused, as if she had switched to a new pair of glasses, and couldn't tell who they were. When she had finally figured out who they were, she simply frowned and asked, 'Why not stay a little longer?' Mrs Lou was so busy today, she felt she had every right to frown as much as she wanted.

Since the Lou family was a 'modern' family, they only invited a few close relatives to the evening banquet, and there weren't any rowdy wedding-night pranks. The next day, the new couple went back to the groom's family for lunch. The bride's parents and siblings were also there. They already had proofs of the wedding pictures. In one, Yuqing stood there alone, her white gown stiffly starched and ironed, her body tilted forward at a precarious angle; she looked like a paper doll propped up on a cardboard stand. There was one of her with Dalu in which her veil was over her face. Her features were indistinct, as if the shadow of a vengeful ghost had accidentally been captured on film. Yuqing was greatly dissatisfied with the pictures and decided that she would rent the gown again and have her pictures retaken.

After lunch, Xiaobo discussed world affairs with himself. In the throes of his eloquence, he stood up to gesticulate and banged his hand on the table. Mrs Lou was sitting on the sofa with the in-laws and her daughter-in-law. She calmly stretched her legs and looked at her lilac stockings, rolled below her knees. She then noticed that no one was really listening; they were passing the wedding pictures around. Now and again, someone yawned. Mrs Lou felt a sudden surge of disgust, but she didn't know whether it was disgust for her husband or for those watching them act like a couple.

The bride's mother wanted to smoke, and Mrs Lou reached over to get the lighter. The midday sun shone on the glass-topped table. The rose-coloured embroidered shoe upper under the glass glittered. Mrs Lou's hand and heart rested awhile over

79

that brilliance. She suddenly remembered that when she was little, she used to stand in front of her house watching the wedding processions: the bridal palanquins and the bands, striking up their relentless and barbaric pipe and gong music, muffling the weeping of the bride. The sound of drums and gongs made the heart quake. In the heat of the noonday sun, colourful tassels from the palanquin – a row of light green, a row of pink, a row of deep red – row upon row rippled in the wind like waves – making your head spin and then bringing the clarity of the noonday sun, like the strong yellow wine one drinks at Dragon Boat Festival. A palanquin bearer's patched short blue trousers showed beneath his embroidered jacket. From above the jacket stuck out his skinny, yellow neck, shiny with sweat, like a maggot squirming out of a jar. The palanquin bearers and the band marched in rows, swaggering extravagantly and colourfully, and the spectators were also immersed in the procession. Everybody was caught up in an immense sense of joy outside themselves that left them reeling.

After all these years, Mrs Lou still remembered. Since she was married and even her eldest son was now married, she should have known that marriage was nothing like that. The weddings she had witnessed as a child gave her a feeling of wholeness. Somehow, her son's celebration hadn't come together. She did not know why that was.

Her husband suddenly ended his discussion of current affairs. Resting his elbow on the mantelpiece, he gave his daughter-in-law a sideways glance and, in the most progressive and scientific tone of voice befitting a new-style father, he asked, 'How does it feel to be married? It's all right, is it?'

Yuqing hesitated a little, then, with all the aplomb she could command, she replied, 'It's fine.' After she had said that, she blushed.

They all laughed, but were slightly ill at ease, not certain if they should have laughed or not. Mrs Lou knew that her husband had made a joke, but she didn't really catch what he said, so she laughed the loudest.

*Translated by Janet Ng (with Janice Wickeri)*

# STEAMED OSMANTHUS
FLOWER: AH XIAO'S
UNHAPPY AUTUMN

Autumn is a song. On nights of 'steamed osmanthus flower' it is like a flute melody played in a kitchen. In the daytime, it is a song sung by small children: ardent and familiar and clear and moist.*

Fatima Mohideen

Leading her son Baishun by the hand, Ding Ah Xiao climbed the stairs, one floor after another. Out beyond the rear balconies of the tall apartment building, the city became a vast open wilderness, an endless blur of innumerable red and grey roofs with backyards, back windows, back alleyways everywhere. Even the sky – now a gloomy, featureless expanse – had turned its face away. The Mid-Autumn Festival had been and gone but the weather was still so hot – what on earth was it up to? Sounds floated up from below: the noise of vehicles of various kinds, of rugs being beaten, of school bells being rung, of workmen banging and sawing, of motors humming. Yet it was all indistinct, as if none of it mattered in the slightest to God, being of no more importance than a gust of wind.

The amah of the apartment directly opposite took her

* Translator's Note: The fragrance of the osmanthus flower is synonymous with autumn. 'Steamed' refers both to the heat and the humidity of an oppressive Indian summer. The title is also a metaphor for the heroine, who is past her prime.

children out on to the rear balcony to eat their congee. The weather was very hot and the congee so scalding that she blew on it with pursed lips, frowning as she did so. But it was hard to tell which she was worried about more: her mouth or the snow-white congee. The neighbour's amah was a yellow-faced woman who had once bound her feet. Her hair, however, was cropped fashionably short. She was busy giving the boys their breakfast and getting them ready for school. A fine, short lock of hair hung down alongside each of her ears. These were so damp they looked like wet paint on her face. She exchanged greetings with Ah Xiao: 'Good morning, Little Sister!' The children chorused: 'Good morning, Auntie!' Ah Xiao replied: 'Good morning, Big Sister!' with Baishun adding, 'Auntie! Big Brothers!'

Ah Xiao said, 'I'm running late this morning. The blasted tram was jam-packed like a can of sardines and I wasn't able to get off until we'd gone past my stop. I'm sure a foreigner must have pressed the bell!'

The neighbour's amah replied, 'This weather's gone crazy. It's so hot!'

Ah Xiao said, 'You can say that again! And it's nearly the ninth month and all!'

Just now in the third-class compartment of the tram, she had been jostled about so much she had barely managed to keep her feet. She had had her face pressed right up close against a tall man's deep-blue gown. Because it was so filthy, the cloth had a peculiar softness about it. It didn't look like cloth at all. Waves of heat emanated from its blue depths. This weather smelled just like that gown – but not one's own clothes, absolutely not. One's own dirt was a lot easier to live with.

Ah Xiao hurriedly opened the door with her key and went inside, going straight to the box that housed the electric bell.

Sure enough, the plaque for number two had fallen off. Her employer had not eaten at home last night and had let her finish two hours earlier. It was her guess that today he would go out of his way to make life bumpy for her, just to even the score. She removed the lid of the water vat and filled the kettle using an iron ladle. She then put the kettle on the gas-stove to boil. Since it was wartime, restrictions applied to the supply of water. Every household had a vat like this one, large and soy-sauce brown with a pale yellow dragon painted on it. Any woman gazing at her own reflection in the water would have seen herself as a classic beauty, but Ah Xiao was a woman of the metropolis who preferred to look at herself in a small chipped makeup mirror (it had come as an accessory in a handbag). This was stuck on the green wall by the door. She examined her hair; it wasn't very fluffy. She wore it in a plait, tightly twisting together small clumps of hair until she could no longer see it. Only then did she feel neat and tidy. Her fringe was tightly permed in the latest style and only needed brushing every three or four days. She took down her white apron from behind the door and tied it on. Then she carried over a bench, stepped up on to it and reached out for the coffee. She was born to be short.

'Baishun! Where's that child got to now? This is no time to think about playing. Come and have your breakfast and then get yourself off to school!' she scolded. Her beautiful, bony face was as stern as a stepmother's when she was angry; Baishun had a round face with small eyes and eyebrows. Trying his best not to annoy his mother, he shifted a bench out through the door, then carried over a biscuit barrel in his arms. He sat down on the barrel, put his cup and his plate on the bench and waited quietly. From a crockery jar on top of the refrigerator, Ah Xiao took out half a loaf of leftover bread and said, 'Here! Take this!

Eat it all up if you can! It'd be nice to leave some for somebody else. No one would ever guess that a mite like you could eat more than a grown-up!'

There was a blue glass on the sill. She took the toothbrush out of it, filled it with water from the thermos flask, and handed it to Baishun, then continued her harangue: 'You expect me to do everything for you! How much are you paying me a month to be your servant? I don't know what I owed you in my last life to deserve this! Hurry up now, it's time to get going!'

Baishun still had his mouth full. As he went to get his schoolbag, he felt suddenly tired of wearing the dirty, blue overalls he had worn all summer and asked: 'Mum, can I wear a jumper tomorrow?' Ah Xiao replied, 'What's got into you? A jumper, for Heaven's sake! In this weather!'

After Baishun had gone, she sighed and thought about how hard it was to cope with the demands of the child's school. Fees had risen considerably and there were all sorts of additional expenses. The cost of the coloured paper and foil she had to buy for his art and craft classes was itself shocking enough. A soy-sauce bottle on the windowsill weighed down a small flag he had made, a slender piece of bamboo poked through the national colours – blue for the sky, white for the sun and red for the earth. Ah Xiao turned to look at it for a moment; the sight of it made her miserable.

The coffee was made and she had just finished arranging the breakfast things neatly on a large silver tray when the telephone rang. Ah Xiao picked up the receiver and spoke into it in sharp, self-important English, 'Hel-lo. Ye-s Mis-s. Plea-se wai-t a mo-ment.' She had not heard this woman's voice before. Another new one. She went and knocked on his door: 'Tele-phone, Sir!'

Her employer was already washed, groomed and dressed.

He looked distinctly annoyed with her. The flesh on his face was like undercooked meat, bright red with traces of blood. Of late, he'd taken to cultivating an abbreviated moustache. This made his face look like a particularly nourishing egg which had already begun to hatch open to reveal a pair of tiny yellow wings. Nevertheless, Mr Garter still passed for a handsome man. There was something extremely artful about his grey eyes, and he carried himself with aplomb. He walked over to the telephone and cleared his throat before answering it, but a slight hoarseness remained. After an interrogative 'Hello?' he immediately dropped his voice to a whisper that conveyed mingled surprise and delight: *'Oh, hello!'* Beside himself with joy, this was the same as saying, 'Could it be true? Is that really you?' Even after rising so early he still knew how to turn on the charm.

Ah Xiao, on the other hand, had heard this seductive *Oh, hello!* countless times before and so withdrew into the kitchen. Yesterday the Blonde had thrown a party. Afterwards she had presumably accompanied him back here – there were two unwashed wineglasses in the kitchen, one kissed with lipstick. What time she had left was anybody's guess. None of his women actually ever stayed the night. After she had left, he'd gone back into the kitchen and eaten a raw egg. Ah Xiao had noticed the intact eggshell in the Western-style rubbish bin. After pricking a small hole in it, he had sucked out its contents. Ah Xiao shook her head. He was nothing but a savage! There was no electricity for the refrigerator now and so it should not have been left shut, but after taking out his egg he had closed the door. She was assailed by a sweet, fetid stink as soon as she opened it. She took out the cheese, pâté and an egg. Except for breakfast which he ate at home, Garter generally accepted invitations to dine out for his other meals. There was still half a bowl of uneaten fried rice in the refrigerator. It had been there for more than a week already. She knew that he hadn't forgotten about it because he frequently opened the refrigerator to check its contents. If he didn't take the trouble to say 'I don't want it. You finish it up' she wasn't going to ask him 'Do you still want it?' She knew what he was like.

After hanging up the telephone, her employer checked the memorandum book for a telephone number Ah Xiao had written down for someone who had called while he was out. He dialled the number accordingly but could not get through. Sticking his head in through the kitchen door, he called to her, drawing out his words: 'Amah, this is embarrassing. Why can't you ever get the numbers right!' He pointed a finger and shook it disapprovingly. Ah Xiao twisted her hands in her apron, a reddening grin bright on her face.

He glanced down at her son's leftover bread. Ah Xiao sensed his suspicion. She had in fact bought the bread with a ration-ticket given to her by the Mrs next door. Before her employer said a word, she had flushed bright red. Suzhou amahs are a proud lot and are upset by the merest show of displeasure on the part of their employers, let alone a reprimand. Ah Xiao was particularly vulnerable. As soon as she blushed it looked as if she had been slapped in the face. Red welts like fingermarks rose on her thin cheeks. The whole shape of her face gave her a look of suffering. Her fine eyes were like two long slits, and the distant world revealed in them was one of classical beauty that was capable of 'charming geese and fishes while shaming moon and flowers'.

Her employer was thinking to himself: 'Finding a replacement for her would be difficult. I'll keep in her good books for as long as she's in my employment.' For this reason he didn't question her about the bread. Instead he said: 'Amah, you will serve dinner for two tonight. Buy a pound of beef.' Ah Xiao asked: 'Shall I make soup with the meat first and then fry it, Sir?' Her employer nodded. Ah Xiao then asked: 'Anything else, Sir?' Her employer stood there thinking to himself, one hand propped against the frame of the door, the other pressed on his hip. When he wasn't giving women flirtatious looks, those grey eyes of his grew large and staring, their whites exposed. He glared at the leftover bread, making Ah Xiao feel uncomfortable. 'Corn, perhaps,' he suggested. She nodded and said: 'Corn, Sir.' It was the same thing every time. Fortunately, she thought, the guest was always a different woman. He continued: 'I'd like a dessert as well. A couple of pancakes would do nicely.' Ah Xiao replied: 'There's no flour, Sir.' He said: 'Make them with eggs, then. You don't need flour.' Ah Xiao had never in her life heard of anyone serving up sweetened egg but assented readily: 'Yes, Sir.'

She brought out breakfast, and noticed that the photograph of the Blonde had been removed from the small cabinet. Tonight's guest was presumably the new woman. He was never willing to take away the photograph when Miss Li and her like came to dinner. Miss Li was very considerate. She gave Ah Xiao a hundred dollars every time she visited. Ah Xiao thought she might be the concubine of some very rich family, but she could not say for sure: she seemed to enjoy more freedom and was not pretty enough – although of course not all concubines were beautiful.

Ah Xiao answered another telephone call: 'Hel-lo? . . . Ye-s Mis-s. Plea-se wai-t a mo-ment.' She knocked and went in: 'Telephone, Sir.' Her employer asked who it was. 'Miss Li,' she replied. Her employer did not wish to speak with her and so she had to put the caller off: 'Mr Garter . . . *she's* in the bath!' Ah Xiao could only pronounce 'hello' with any degree of accuracy; anything after that came out rather muddled. She had never quite grasped the difference between *he* and *she*. 'I'm sorry, Miss. Perhaps you could call back later?' To the 'Thank you' on the other end of the line she responded: 'Don't mention it. Goodbye, Miss.'

Mr Garter went to the office after breakfast. Before leaving, he had as usual bid her a charming farewell from the front door: 'Goodbye, Amah!' He was determined to make women like him, regardless of who they were. Ah Xiao came out smiling and replied: 'Goodbye, Sir!' She went in to tidy up. As she walked into the bathroom, she could not help gritting her teeth in anger. Mr Garter had put all the sheets, pillowcases, shirts, pants, and small and large towels in the bath to soak, worried that she wasn't going to do all the washing in one go. But there was no sun today; how on earth was she going to get everything dry and do the shopping as well? Running water in the apart-ment was available for only one hour a day, but with the bathtub full of clothes she would miss this opportunity. Yet he insisted on a daily bath.

Miss Li called a second time. Ah Xiao said: 'Mr Garter . . . *she's* gone to the office!' Switching into Chinese, Miss Li asked her for his telephone number at work. Doing likewise, Ah Xiao replied: 'This is Miss Li I'm speaking to, isn't it?' She laughed, her whole face flushing bright red with the embarrassment she felt for her on behalf of all decent women. 'I don't know his number at the office . . . He didn't go out yesterday . . . Yes, he ate dinner at home . . . He dined alone. I'm not sure about tonight. He hasn't said anything about it . . .'

Then the Blonde rang. She wanted to send somebody round with the plates and cutlery she had borrowed from Garter for her big party the night before. Ah Xiao replied: 'Mr Garter . . . *she's* gone to the office! . . . Yes, Mis-s. This is Amah speaking

. . . I'm very well, thank you Mis-s.' The voice of the Blonde was as sweet as a toffeed candy-twist, and everything she said was coated with affected friendliness. Ah Xiao's responses were similarly false. With her shy laughter she seemed unable to bridge the social gap between them. She asked: 'What time will you be sending the amah round? I'm about to go to the market and probably won't be back until 9.30 . . . Thank you, Mis-s . . . Don't mention it. Goodbye, Mis-s.' She made her voice sharp and shrill, emitting a series of crackling sounds. The world of foreign language was always happy, well-to-do, founded on sand.

She went out, did her shopping, and returned to the apartment. Xiuqin, the Blonde's amah, was a younger friend of hers; it was Ah Xiao who had asked Mr Garter to recommend her. She knocked at the back door and called out: 'Big Sis! Big Sis!' Xiuqin was only twenty-one or -two, of strong build; she wore her hair long and curly. She didn't seem to feel the heat: over her blue chemise she wore a jade-green angora jacket. It was obviously a rare blessing to be able to dress like a university student. The two small, reddened eyes set in her large, round face were more closed than open (was she perhaps suffering from trachoma?) and she seemed to show an awareness of this unusual distinction, looking out at the world like a Mongolian woman peering through the heavy, brightly coloured tassels which covered her face.

Ah Xiao took a stack of plates wrapped in newspaper from her, and asked, smiling: 'What time did they finish up last night then?' Xiuqin replied: 'They were carrying on until two or three in the morning.' Ah Xiao commented: 'Your Mrs came over here afterwards and didn't leave until some time after daybreak.' Xiuqin replied: 'She came over here, did she?' Ah Xiao said, 'Well, it seems she did.' As they gossiped about these things, they smiled with a special innocence as if they weren't discussing the affairs of other people at all. Their male employers were like the wind, rushing about helter-skelter, blowing up dust, while the women resembled the ornate carvings on expensive furniture, so particularly attractive to dust that they were kept busy cleaning from morning to night. Their grumbling, however, had nothing to do with this.

Xiuqin held her arms crossed before her breasts, looking on as Ah Xiao tidied the crockery away. She rambled on as if speaking to herself: 'My mistress and your master are two of a kind. When it comes to money they sure know how to spend up big, but they're not willing to part with a cent for everyday expenses. The other night when she had guests over, we were a few chairs short, so she asked the people across from us if she could have a loan of some of theirs. When there wasn't enough bread, she made do by borrowing a bowl of rice from the neighbours.' Ah Xiao responded: 'Well, compared to our Master, she's a bit more generous. We've never had people over for dinner parties, only solitary women, and I'll tell you what they get to eat: beef boiled up to make soup followed by the same piece of beef fried and served as a separate dish. Then there's corn. And if it's her first time, she also gets a dessert, but never the second time . . . He's got this Miss Li who can't get used to eating such food so she gets a restaurant to deliver here. Miss Li really cares about him! Now he's gone and found himself another new one. I think he's getting less and less choosy: each one's worse than the last. This new one can't even pronounce his name.' Xiuqin asked: 'Is she Chinese?' Ah Xiao nodded: 'Even the Chinese have their different levels . . . Little Sis, come and have a look at this set of silver bowl and chopsticks Miss Li gave him for his birthday. She knows how much he likes Chinese things so she had them specially made by a jeweller.

They come in a glass case decorated with a red paper-cut of the word for "longevity".' Xiuqin looked at the gift, clicking her tongue and sighing: 'They must have cost a few thousand, I reckon.' Ah Xiao replied: 'And the rest!'

By this time the sun had come out a little and shone into the room like a blue haze the shade of cigarette smoke. Colourful silk cushions lay scattered on the bed. There was a wireless and some illustrated magazines on the bed-head. By the bed there was a pair of slippers, a small blue-and-red Peking rug, a waste-paper basket in the shape of a palace lantern, and a set of carved tables of different sizes neatly stacked one inside the other. Hanging on the wall was a Peking opera mask; on the table, a pair of tin candle-holders. The knick-knacks which filled the room made it look somewhat like the boudoir of a high-class White Russian prostitute who had gathered together some Chinese odds and ends to build herself a nest of peace and happiness. Most exquisite of all were the smoky-purple glasses arranged on top of a small cabinet. They came in various shapes and sizes for different sorts of drinks. There was an orderly row of bottles sealed with large wooden egg-shaped stoppers lacquered red and blue and green. And then in the bathroom there was a whole set of light yellow-grey glass combs, seven or eight in all, arranged according to the fineness of their teeth. The sight of these made one's heart ache with sadness because the Master had already begun to lose his hair. The more he worried about it, the more those precious strands became like eyelashes to him: prone to fall out at the slightest touch.

On the wall there was an advertisement for a brand of Western spirits enclosed in a narrow silver frame. Leaning in the darkness was a naked beauty of astonishing proportions with red hair and fair skin. The caption read: 'The best in town', rating her as highly as this particular brand of whiskey. She was resting one arm on an invisible piece of furniture for support and it looked very uncomfortable, stiffly propping up her entire frame. She was a real Snow Queen, her body like a Popsicle with sinews of ice congealed on its surface. She tilted herself to highlight her large, turned-up breasts, her exaggeratedly slim waist and her tapering thighs. Her feet were bare, but she was doing her best to balance on the very tips of her toes as if standing in high heels. She had the face of a child, squat and square, and large brown eyes indicating neither pleasure nor voluptuousness that gazed out blankly at her viewers beyond the frame. She was like a small child being photographed in new clothes. There wasn't even a trace of pride in her look. She wore her trim suit of armour – her magnificent breasts, her thighs, her bouffant hair – like a fashion model parading a store's garments for the customers to admire.

This was Mr Garter's ideal. But he had as yet never met her in the flesh. Had he done so, he would have only tried to gain some slight advantage by her. If it involved too much trouble, it wouldn't have been worth it. He himself was a mature beauty, and had become more and more economical with time and money as he grew older. Moreover, it was now clear to him that women were all more or less the same. He had always believed in making relationships with women of good families, or with ladies of the *demi-monde* in search of a little romance outside working hours. He didn't expect them to rob the rich for his benefit; all he wanted was an equitable exchange. He knew that 'long-term gamblers had to lose, just as long-time lovers had their blues'. At the gaming table he always checked to see which way the wind was blowing and, if things were favourable, took advantage of the situation to make a bit of a profit. But he always knew when to stop.

There was nothing obscene about the photo-like painting on

the wall. It was the equivalent of a streamlined sports car in a showroom: worth a look even if you weren't in the market to buy. Ah Xiao and Xiuqin avoided looking at it directly, unwilling to give the impression that they were from the country and therefore easily shocked by such things.

Ah Xiao said: 'I should do this tub of washing while there's still water. Sit down and rest a moment, Sister. To think there are such infatuated women in this world!' she said, still thinking of Miss Li as she bent over kneading the wet clothes, and panting as she spoke. 'Why should she take a fancy to him?! The man is pettier than ten women put together! The Mrs next door was given an extra ration-ticket for bread and so gave it to me to buy a loaf. But he thought it was his. You should have seen the way he stared at it. Even if I had to steal, I wouldn't steal from him! There are some leftovers from last week but if he won't come out and say he doesn't want them I'm not going to touch anything that belongs to him. He says: "Shanghai's a terrible place! Even the Chinese servants cheat foreigners!" But if he wasn't in Shanghai, he would have been killed off long ago in the foreigners' own war. It was like this last time. He filled the bathtub with clothes and left them to soak, afraid I wasn't going to wash them. The colour of the shirts ran, making a real mess, but he never said a word about it. I think he's getting cheaper and cheaper. This woman he's seeing tonight . . . It's no wonder he catches those diseases! In the last couple of months he's had these sores like boils all over his head and face. He's much better now, but that medicine he was using made a mess of the sheets.'

Xiuqin hadn't said a word for a long time. When Ah Xiao turned around, she found her leaning against the door, biting on a finger and deep in thought. Ah Xiao then remembered that the family of her husband-to-be wanted them to be married.

Her mother had come to take her back to the country but she didn't want to go. She asked: 'Is your mother still in Shanghai?' Xiuqin responded with a rush of intimacy: 'Oh, Sis. I can't bear it!' She was on the verge of weeping. Her gentle eyes, red and moist with tears, looked exactly like lips.

Ah Xiao said: 'I think you'll have to go back. Otherwise, people will gossip. "Such a grown-up girl," they'll say, "she must be up to something in Shanghai."' Xiuqin replied: 'That's what Mother says! I'll have to go, but I'll come back right away. I could never get used to living in the country! In the last few days Mother has been running around buying this and that and complaining no end about the cost of things. I told her, "What are you making such a fuss about? You only bought these quilts and pillows to show off, and as for those embroidered clothes, I'll never be able to wear them in Shanghai." I couldn't care less about anything else but they must give me a gold ring. By rights that is what they have to do. You wait and see. If they try to give me one that's only gold-plated, I'm going to throw it away! Just see if I don't!'

This display of pride displeased Ah Xiao somewhat. She and her husband had not had a proper marriage ceremony. All these years she had regretted her decision to move in with him without going through all the excitement of a wedding. She said: 'In fact, you'd be better off making a few compromises. Things aren't like they used to be. Where on earth do you expect them to lay their hands on gold?' She had intended to make a few rather icy remarks but couldn't manage it. Bent over the bathtub, the heat stupefied her. The perspiration on her upper lip stung, and sweat trickled down from her scalp. When she wiped her head with her hand she was surprised by just how much she was sweating. She squatted low on the floor, and Xiuqin could smell the wafts of sweat rising up from her black glazed-silk shirt, acrid as the crisp, fishy smell a watermelon has when it is sliced open.

Xiuqin heaved another sigh: 'I suppose I can't not go! The floor of their home is earthen, but they have laid a proper one in our bedroom . . . The worry is killing me! I've heard the man likes to gamble. Sis, what do you think I should do?'

After wringing the water out of the washing, Ah Xiao took it out to dry on the front balcony. Baishun had come home from school, but not daring to ring the doorbell, waited outside the back door, calling 'Mum! Mum!' as he banged on the wooden railing. Beyond the apartment building, the pale city looked even more deserted under the midday sun. Ah Xiao didn't hear him until she had hung out all the clothes and returned to the kitchen to start lunch. As she opened the door and let him in she scolded: 'Why are you making such a racket? You couldn't wait, could you!'

She asked Xiuqin to stay and eat with them; in addition, two guests turned up. One was an elderly lady from their home village who liked to chat with Ah Xiao. This was the only time in the day she was free and, since she didn't want to put anyone to any trouble, she brought along her own cold rice in a basket, patiently climbing up eleven flights of stairs. The other, another 'Sister', carried rice and did temporary work. It was Ah Xiao who had found her a job doing the laundry for a family on the next floor down. She looked at Baishun and asked: 'So this is your boy, is it?' 'Say hello to your "auntie",' Ah Xiao bawled at Baishun, blushing as she turned to her friends as if she owed them an apology: 'He looks like a little tramp, doesn't he?'

In times such as these, Ah Xiao didn't often invite guests to stay for lunch with such warmth. She liked to put up a good front, and was pleased that she happened to have rice. As she fried the food, the elderly woman began questioning Xiuqin about the preparations for her dowry. Xiuqin smiled but could hardly get a word out, blushing like a bride. Ah Xiao answered every question on her behalf, and the old woman made numerous suggestions.

The short-term worker asked: 'That couple that's just moved into the upstairs apartment in your building – are they newly-weds too?' Ah Xiao replied: 'Ah-hah. They bought that apartment for 1.5 million. His family's got money. So does hers. They put on a real show! The apartment, the furniture, several dozen sets of bedding, as well as ten piculs of rice and the same amount of coal! I don't know where they're going to find space for everything in an apartment like that! Four servants accompanied the bride: a male and female domestic, a cook and a trishaw-puller.' The four servants looked like the paper dolls used in funeral services; they stood ram-rod straight, as neat and tidy as can be. People with money really knew how to do things in style! Ah Xiao began to cheer up. All this talk eclipsed Xiuqin entirely: even her anxieties seemed to pale into insignificance.

The short-term worker then asked: 'How many days have they been married?' Ah Xiao replied: 'About three altogether, I think.' The elderly woman asked: 'And was it a new-style wedding or an old-style one?' Ah Xiao answered: 'New style, of course. But there was also a trousseau: I saw them carrying box after box up the stairs.' Xiuqin chimed in with a question of her own: 'Is the bride pretty?' Ah Xiao replied: 'I haven't actually seen the bride. They don't go out at all and things upstairs are always quiet. I never hear a peep out of them.' The short-term worker commented: 'I saw her when they came to inspect the apartment. She was quite fat and wore glasses.' As if jumping to her defence, Ah Xiao replied with annoyance: 'Perhaps that wasn't the bride you saw after all.'

Leaning against the door frame and holding her bowl of food

in her hands, the elderly woman sighed: 'We're better off working for the foreigners. Everything is spelled out clearly!' Ah Xiao said: '*Aiya!* These days, I'd rather get paid less. At least you had enough to eat and somewhere to live working for Chinese families. Someone like me earns 3,000 dollars a month on paper, but I could spend more than that on food alone! Some employers provide meals even though they're under no obligation to do so. Look at the people who live opposite us, for instance. When they eat potatoes they always fry up half a basinful and so the servants get their share too.' Baishun said: 'Mum, the people opposite are having dried vegetables and roast meat today.' Ah Xiao put her chopsticks together and hit him with the thick ends, scolding: 'If they eat so well, why don't you go and join them? Well, why don't you? Huh? Why don't you?' Baishun blinked but did not cry, the others all doing their best to console him. The short-term worker said: 'I've got two little tramps of my own, but although they're older, they're not nearly as clever as this one!' She came up to him and said affectionately: 'Tramp!' trying to make him forget his upset. 'Why aren't you eating your rice? You've polished off most of the vegetables, but you've still got a bowlful of rice there!' Softening towards her son, Ah Xiao said: 'Leave him be. If he's not allowed to eat whatever he wants at lunch, the next thing you know he'll be asking for a snack.' Then she turned to him and urged: 'Eat all you want while there's still food. There won't be anything else to eat later on even if you kick up a fuss.'

The elderly woman asked Baishun: 'Don't you have to go back to school after lunch?' Ah Xiao explained: 'It's Saturday today.' She turned around and grabbed a hold of Baishun: 'Come Saturday and you vanish as soon as I let you out the door. You sit here quietly and do your revision for a couple of hours before you go out and play.' Baishun sat on the biscuit barrel, his book propped against a bench, rocking from side to side as he read in a sing-song voice: 'I want to grow up big and strong, big and strong! Mummy and Daddy say I'm a good boy, a good boy!' Even before he had read a couple of sentences he asked: 'Mummy, after I've read for two hours I'll go out and play. Mummy, what time is it now?'

Ah Xiao ignored him, but Xiuqin laughed and said: 'Baishun has a good voice. Why don't you send him off to study story-telling, Sister? He could earn a lot of money.' Ah Xiao was speechless for a moment. She blushed, laughed weakly and said: 'He wouldn't be any good at that, would he? He's still got a way to go before he finishes primary school. Although he's not much of a student, I'd still like him to do well at school and have a good future.' Xiuqin replied: 'What grade's he in?' Ah Xiao said: 'Only the third. He repeated a year. It's embarrassing!' She glanced over at Baishun, a widow's sadness welling up in her heart. Although she had a husband, it wasn't much different from being on her own: she had to rely on herself. Her look frightened Baishun, and he rocked with greater speed as he chanted: 'I want to grow up big and strong, big and strong . . .'

The elderly woman said: 'This weather's very strange. Even when it's not a leap month, it usually starts to cool down by now.' Baishun suddenly thought of something and looked up, laughing: 'Mummy, when it gets cold I want to buy a face-mask. The teacher said face-masks are good because you don't catch cold!' This threw Ah Xiao into a rage: 'You've got a nerve with your "Teacher this, Teacher that"! You repeated a year but you're quite pleased with yourself. Pleased with yourself! Pleased!' She struck out at him, hitting him twice. Baishun burst into tears. The elderly woman immediately tried to stop her: 'That's enough. You've hit him twice already.'

Ah Xiao wiped Baishun's runny nose for him and shouted: 'All right, stop crying and get on with your reading!' Baishun read quietly to himself, sobbing as he did so. All of a sudden, he called out in delight: 'Mummy, Daddy's here!' Daddy's arrival always made Mummy happy, and even he shared in the benefits of that. The guests all knew that Ah Xiao's man worked as a tailor, and that because he lived in his shop, the couple rarely had a chance to be together. This made them extremely affectionate towards one another. They all greeted him, made several remarks for the sake of polite conversation, and then said their goodbyes. Ah Xiao saw them to the back door, saying: 'Please come again!' Trailing along behind her, Baishun added: 'Come again, Aunties!'

Ah Xiao's husband wore an old silk gown with a high collar and carried a large white cloth bundle in his arms. Ah Xiao brought over a chair for him to sit down. Although the sun gradually shifted until its light shone on his body, he stayed where he was, hugging his knees in his arms. The fierce afternoon sunlight stuck to the bright kitchen, with its steel pots, metal stove and white ceramic tiles, like a hot baked pancake. Being small, there was nowhere in it to escape from the heat. Ah Xiao set up her ironing board to do the ironing, making things hotter still. She made her man a cup of tea. As a rule, she never used any of her employer's tea-leaves, but she made an exception when her man visited. Clasping his cup in his hands, he sipped his tea, and, with a hint of a smile on his lips, listened to all the things Ah Xiao told him as she ironed. He had a yellowish face, and his dense black hair and eyebrows made him look intelligent. But for some unknown reason, the lower part of his face simply fell away. His bucked teeth were like a hand reaching downwards, pulling his mouth along with it.

She told him all about Xiuqin's marriage, about how she

wouldn't marry without a gold ring, about her extravagance. He would punctuate her remarks with the occasional 'Mmm', his cagey black pupils gazing into his tea and his smile very understanding, sympathetic. This hurt her; it also made her angry. The worry was all hers, it seemed. It didn't make much difference to a man whether he got married or not. At the same time she also felt bored by the whole affair. Their child was a big boy now, so what use was there thinking about such things? It was true he wasn't supporting her, but he probably wouldn't have been able to support her even if they had been legally married. What powers had chosen this life of drudgery for her? He only made enough to cover his own expenses. Sometimes he even asked her for money to pay into his savings club.

The man turned to test his son, pointing to Chinese words in the school reader and asking Baishun what they were. This reminded Ah Xiao of something: 'A letter arrived from my mother today. There are a couple of sentences in it I didn't quite understand.' The words 'Wu County Government' were printed on the envelope and it was addressed to 'Miss Ding Ah Xiao'. In the left-hand corner was written 'Best Wishes'. He read the letter, explaining its contents to her:

My dear daughter Ah Xiao,
I am writing you this letter. Because a couple of days ago you wrote. Here in the country, I know all your news. I think of you in Shanghai, I hope you are in the best of health, and all is well with you. In your letter, you said you are coming back to visit in the tenth month. Very good. Please bring me some Three Days Headache Powder when you come. Very important. Don't forget. Lately, all is quiet here. I am doing well, don't worry about me. I also ask you to bring a woollen jumper for my mother. Don't

forget. If you are not coming, get someone else to bring it. Don't break promise. I'll stop now. We can talk when you come.

Your mother, Wang Yuzhen
14th Ninth Month

There had never been any mention of her man in letters from her home town. Ah Xiao often had Baishun write back on her behalf; there was never any expression of concern for him either. After reading the letter, Ah Xiao and her husband felt somewhat cut-off. He sat there in silence. Suddenly, as if trying to justify himself, he began to speak about his work: 'As well as making clothes, I'm now doing a bit of business in leather goods. These days, you've got to be versatile to make a go of it.' He opened his bundle and pulled out two leather overcoats for her to have a look at, then took out a kind of bag made of fur and said: 'For this reason the sea otter . . .' and began a story about the life and habits of the sea otter which was really intended for Baishun. Baishun was playing up to him. He had left off his reading long ago and was now cuddled up next to Ah Xiao, clinging to her, one hand rummaging around in her pocket. Ah Xiao listened to her husband with rapt attention: 'Mmm . . . Mmm . . . Aha . . . Oh . . . Ah . . .' Her man came to the end of his tale: 'And so you see, the sea is full of weird and wonderful things.' Ah Xiao couldn't think of an appropriate response right away. She wondered for a moment and said: 'There's a lot of cuttlefish for sale at the market at the moment.' He replied: 'Hmm. Cuttlefish are strange things too. You haven't seen those giant cuttlefish. They're bigger than a man and look like a spider with all their legs . . .' Ah Xiao wrinkled up her face and said: 'Really? How disgusting!' She then turned to Baishun and said: 'What are you muttering about? . . . What did you say? . . . I can't hear you . . . Are you kidding? . . . Where am I going to get five dollars from?' Nevertheless, she felt in her pockets and gave him the money.

When she had finished her ironing, Ah Xiao mixed up some batter and made pancakes, using the rationed flour and sugar which she and Baishun were entitled to. Her man felt as if he had been given a treat he hadn't deserved, and followed her around everywhere with his hands clasped behind his back trying to make conversation. Father and son ate first while the pancakes were hot; she went on with her cooking. Hot yellow sunlight shone on their three faces. A cicada landed on the broken bamboo blind out on the rear balcony. Although summer was over it had somehow managed to survive and took advantage of the heat, happily chirping its loud and resonant *chua-chua-chua!*

Her employer returned, and as he passed by the kitchen door, he stuck his head in and called to her tenderly: 'Hello, Amah!' Her man had already retreated to the rear balcony, taking in the scenery with his hands folded behind his back. Garter spent 3,000 dollars on hiring a servant and was only too anxious to have her flapping and pecking around his head like a tame pigeon on his return. He kept ringing the bell for her until he had her running in circles. As she was taking ice out of the refrigerator, her man came behind her and said in a low voice: 'I'll come over tonight.' Ah Xiao replied resentfully: 'We'll die in this heat!' The room she shared with Baishun was like a steam-cooker. But then she suddenly sensed him standing there, so lonely on his own. He wasn't in the habit of asking for favours – at least, he had never asked her to do anything. She stood facing the silver-grey ribcage of the refrigerator. She understood nothing of its workings – it was like an X-ray photograph of the human body – but she could hear the heavy pounding of its heart. Waves of cold made her nose hurt and she wanted to cry. Without turning around she remarked: 'Baishun had better spend the night with the people opposite. Their amah lives there with her children.' 'Hmm,' he replied.

After she had delivered the ice to her employer, she found that her man had gone. She went downstairs to fetch two buckets of water for her employer's bath. The doorbell rang. It was the new woman, as expected. Ah Xiao guessed she was a taxi-dancer. 'Is the foreigner at home?' she asked, jiggling her way into the apartment. A great clump of curly hair stuck out from the back of her head; it was dry and yellow from overperming, while the rest of her hair was black. It looked like a fur collar wrapped round her neck, the pelt of some dead animal. In this case it was hard to say for sure that it was actually dead. It seemed to quiver, jumping with every step she took.

Ah Xiao took in the cocktails and biscuits. Miss Li called again on the telephone. Ah Xiao told her that her employer was not at home. This time, Miss Li could not contain her resentment and interrogated Ah Xiao: 'Did you tell him I rang this morning?' Ah Xiao also lost her temper. No one had ever doubted her professional integrity before. She replied with faint laughter: 'Of course I did! Perhaps he forgot. Didn't he call you later?' Miss Li paused for a moment and then answered: 'No, he didn't' in a very faint voice. Ah Xiao thought to herself: You asked for it. Fancy being told off by a servant! But when she remembered the hundred dollars Miss Li gave her every time she visited, she proffered a gracious explanation on Mr Garter's behalf. Regardless of whether Miss Li believed it or not, it spared her something of the embarrassment. 'He got up late today and left in a hurry for the office. With all the work he has to do and all the people he has to deal with, I'm afraid it's not convenient for him to call . . .' Miss Li responded with a 'Hmm, hmm' on the other end of the line but she sounded as though she were now crying. Ah Xiao said: 'When he gets back I'll tell him that you rang . . .' In a voice that came from far, far away, Miss Li said indistinctly: 'Don't mention anything to him . . .' But then she added: 'I'll call again in a few days' time when I'm free.' It seemed that she couldn't even let go of this lowly amah, whom she started to engage in small talk. She had noticed last time she called that the fitted sheet on Garter's bed needed mending. Seeing he was a bachelor and had no one to take care of him, she was thinking of making him a new one. At this point, Ah Xiao began to find Miss Li's fussiness somewhat repellent and she rose to her employer's defence: 'Oh, he's been planning to get a new one for some time. When he bought the apartment, the bed came with it, but it has never been very suitable. All along he's been thinking of buying a bigger one. If you make a cover for this bed, it will be the wrong size. I recently mended it for him and it looks fine now.' She suddenly felt a motherly protectiveness towards Garter that was both firm and ferocious.

As she was speaking, Mr Garter stuck his head out the door to see what was going on. Flustered, Ah Xiao said to Miss Li: 'Why, that sounds like the lift. I can't be sure, but it might be him coming now!' With one hand covering the receiver she told Mr Garter who it was. Garter frowned, walked over to the telephone, pointed in the direction of the inner room and told Ah Xiao to go in and remove the wineglasses. He picked up the receiver and remained standing for the time being, leaning against the wall with one hand on his hip. On his guard, he asked: 'Hello . . . Yes, I've been extremely busy these last few days . . . Now don't be silly. It's not like that.' There was no explosion on the other end of the line. Even her sobbing was concealed by an intake of breath. He relaxed, and repeated gaily in a low voice: 'Don't be silly . . . How are you, anyway?' Twittering on like this was best just in case the other woman was listening in. 'I've already had him buy those shares for you. See how lucky you are! Have you had one of your headaches recently? And how have you been sleeping? . . .' He blew into the telephone twice, making her ears tickle terribly. Perhaps in the past he had often playfully blown into her ears like this. Both of them appeared to be reliving the sweet experiences of days gone by. There was loud laughter. Then he continued: 'Well, when can I see you?' At the mention of a meeting, he became very businesslike; his tone instantly stiffening, intent on precision. 'What about Friday? . . . How about this: come over to my place first, then we'll decide.' If she comes to his place first, that means they definitely won't go out anywhere; they'll eat at home instead. With one hand he untangled the twisted cord of the telephone while bending down to read the wrongly written telephone numbers Ah Xiao had taken down in the memorandum book on the table. She always wrote the number '9' upside down. Who was it then who had called? Could it have been . . . Oh, this amah was impossible! He spoke abruptly into the telephone: 'No, I have to go out tonight. I only came back to change before going out . . .' But then he softened again: a telephone conversation should end on a lingering note. He said: 'So . . . until Friday!' with a hint of a sigh, and then urged: 'Take care. Bye-bye, my sweet!' The last phrase sounded like a gentle kiss.

Ah Xiao went in to gather up the glasses on the cane table out on the balcony where the woman was leaning on the railing. All this was probably so fresh and romantic for the young taxi-dancer. A layer of mist rose over the twilit city, and rickshaws emerging from the dimness in the far distance seemed to pass at incredibly slow speeds. The lights of cars, the bells of bicycles were diminished, unusually faint, as if Shanghai too had become a Forbidden City.

One corner of a balcony on the floor below jutted out like the prow of a steamship. A young master sat out on it enjoying the cool air, one leg propped up on the railing, chair tilted, rocking backwards and forwards without falling. In one hand he held a tabloid newspaper although it was already too dark to read. Night was falling, and the balcony floor was littered with the remains of persimmons and water chestnuts he had eaten. Ah Xiao felt an overwhelming urge to go and sweep up for him. All around, the night was as black as the bottom of the sea. This dark balcony was a sunken ship laden with faintly shining treasure. In her heart Ah Xiao felt calm and contentment.

She went back to her cooking. Hot oil crackled explosively in the pan as she made herself busy, dashing about like a startled bird. First of all, she carried in an old-style folding kitchen table and spread a tablecloth over it. She brought in the soup and the meat first and then started dessert. Sweetened omelette was just too revolting. In a moment of weakness, she relented and used some of ther own rationed flour to make pancakes for him.

She and Baishun ate doughballs in soup with vegetables. In the pot it looked like a light green paste, quivering as it cooked, its surface wobbling slightly. Baishun finished first and went out on the rear balcony where he recited to himself: 'The moon grows smaller! The stars grow fewer!'

This took Ah Xiao by surprise: 'What's that nonsense you're saying?' she laughed. 'What do you mean "The moon grows smaller! The stars grow fewer!"? You must be mad!'

She went back inside to clean up the dinner things. Her employer told her: 'We're going out in a minute. Get the bed ready after we've left and then you can go.' Ah Xiao assented, but she couldn't help feeling that this was unusual. This woman must have really had her wits about her. At any rate, it looked as if he were prepared to spend a bit more money on her than he had with the others.

She thought she'd wait until she was about to leave before she took Baishun over to her neighbours' amah, otherwise she might think it was too much trouble. She boiled up the kettle twice so that she could wash Baishun's face, neck and feet. The telephone rang and she went to answer it: 'Hel-lo?' There was a long silence on the other end of the line. She gathered that the caller must be Chinese who had dialled the wrong number and so adopted the tone of an aggressive, hot-tempered Western woman, repeating fierily: 'Hel-lo!' The caller responded with a tentative: 'Hello. Is the amah still there?' It was her man. He'd been waiting for her for a long time already. 'It's already ten o'clock,' he told her.

Ah Xiao listened out: not a sound came from her employer's room. Baishun sat dozing on the biscuit barrel. It had begun to rain and the bamboo blind was dripping with water, as if the slats were dreaming of the leaves they once sprouted. She thought: 'That's worked out well. Now I have an excuse.' She woke Baishun and took him over to the neighbours, explaining the situation to the amah: 'It's raining. I can't take him back with me, I'm afraid the child will slip over in the wet. He catches cold easily, too. He's better off spending the night here with his auntie.' When she returned to the apartment, there was still no sign that her employer was about to make a move. Her temper flared. When no one responded to her knock, she quietly pushed open the door a fraction. The room was pitch-black: the pair of them had already slipped out without her knowing. Ah Xiao swallowed down her anger and made the bed ready. She herself got ready to leave, clutching her keys, a string bag and an umbrella. Not wanting to get her knee-length overcoat thoroughly drenched, she folded it inside-out over one arm. Then she opened the back door and went downstairs.

It rained more and more heavily. Suddenly the sky had turned around to show the world its enormous pitch-black face, and everything in this mortal sphere fled away in panic. There was banging and clattering in the darkness, and the thunder and lightning boomed and flashed frenetically. An anguished blue, white and violet lit up the small kitchen time and again. Wind bowed the glass of the window inwards.

Ah Xiao walked two blocks defiantly, but she had no choice but to turn back, trudging her way step by step back up the stairs, fumbling for the lock of the door, opening it, turning on the light with her bag gloved over her hand. Her head and the rest of her body had been drenched by the dark waters. She took off her shoes and socks. The colour in the red flowers embroidered on her white satin shoes had run, bleeding all over the uppers. She squeezed out the water and hung up her shoes to dry on the knobs of the window. Walking around on the tiled floor in her bare feet, she felt as if she were touching her own heart with her hands: it was as cold as a slab of stone. There was no one else in or outside the kitchen; she could have cried aloud if she had wanted to. The unexpected arrival of this insane freedom startled her and made her feel vaguely ill at ease. *I can't stay here on my own. Go and get Baishun this minute.* She went over to her neighbours' place. Fortunately their backdoor was unbolted, and there was still a light on in the kitchen. She went straight in, tapping on the window, calling with a hoarseness in her voice: 'Sister, open up!' The amah replied: 'What? You haven't left yet?' Smiling, Ah Xiao replied: 'The rain was too heavy and there are no lights in that blasted street. The road is full of holes and they were all filled to the brim with water. What a nuisance! I think I'm better off spending the night here. Has that little tramp of mine gone to bed yet? It's best if I take him back with me.' The neighbouring amah asked: 'Do you have a quilt here?' 'Yes, I do,' Ah Xiao replied.

She spread a quilt over the kitchen table, cushioned underneath with newspaper, then turned out the light, so that she and Baishun could try and get some sleep in this makeshift bed. The cramped quality of their warm reunion gave birth to two flies which buzzed around their heads. It was still pouring with rain. There was a sudden flash of lightning, its bluish glare illuminating a spider crawling across the white enamel basin.

The newly-weds upstairs started arguing. There was a loud noise which sounded like someone stamping her feet, or being kicked or pushed back against a kitchen cupboard or the window. Sobbing, the woman ranted on at length in what sounded like Yangzhou dialect: 'Go on, hit me! . . . Hit me! . . . Kill me, I dare you! . . .' Ah Xiao listened attentively, her head on her pillow, thinking to herself: 'They've bought a 1.5-million-dollar apartment so they can fight in it! They've only been married three days. They've got no reason to argue! . . . Unless of course the woman hasn't been completely honest . . .' By some obscure connection she thought of Xiuqin and the family of her future husband who had specially put down a proper floor in what was to be the couple's bedroom. Xiuqin had no choice but to get married.

Upstairs, the argument went on in fits and starts. It flared up again. This time the loud sounds had to be those of the woman opening the French windows. It sounded as if she were preparing to throw herself down into the street but was being restrained by her husband. No longer hurling abuse at him, she merely wailed loudly. The sound of her crying gradually diminished, but the storm outside raged like a high tide, baying mournfully. Later, there was another spate of shouting and crying in the dead still of the night, followed by a burst of howling wind and rain strangely separate from one another like sound effects applied too obviously in a play.

Ah Xiao dragged over a woollen jumper and covered Baishun with it. She remembered how she had once gone to see a film with her son and her husband. The woman in the movie had somehow managed to push open a window and climb through it. Outside in the street it was pouring with rain. She staggered around in the storm, but no matter where she ran to, it poured down on her in torrents. Ah Xiao turned over anxiously. Beyond her pillow, the rain bucketed down towards her head. She fell asleep in the rain.

Around midnight, Garter returned to the apartment with the woman and came into the kitchen to get some ice. As soon as the electric light was switched on, it shone directly on to the large kitchen table. Baishun murmured in his sleep. Ah Xiao woke up, but made out she was still asleep. She was only wearing a singlet and a pair of striped drawers. She lay on her side facing away from the door, her short, thin arms and legs pressed frog-like against Baishun. The two flies left her head and buzzed against the light globe with a tinkling sound. Garter looked her over. In the light of day, this amah was actually extremely pretty and quite charming, but in her underwear she wasn't really much to look at. This thought consoled him because he had never had any intention of getting involved with her: having an affair with a woman from the serving classes would have given her ideas above her station – a most unwise thing to do. Moreover, in extraordinary times such as these, competent servants were difficult to find, while there were plenty of women available for the taking.

Garter went out with a glass bowl filled with ice. In the room, the woman laughed her full laugh, all the alcohol she had drunk sloshing around inside her. She became a gleaming, transparent bottle of wine, a bottle of perfume, an expensive gift item lying in a box on a bed of curled strips of pale-green paper. When the door closed, the laughter became inaudible, but the reek of alcohol and perfume lingered a long time in the air. When the light in the kitchen was turned out, the flies flew aimlessly back to Ah Xiao's head.

The rain had stopped quite some time ago, it seemed. Out on the street, a pedlar selling food cried his wares in a long, drawn-out phrase of four syllables. It wasn't clear what he was selling; all one heard was the prolonged sadness. A drunken party of men and women staggered down the street singing in a foreign language, giggling and laughing as they went. Their song was a form of defiance against the dead weight of the night, but it was flimsy, weak, and would soon vanish. It was the pedlar's cry which filled the entire street, all the cares of the world loaded on the carrying pole he shouldered.

The following day, Ah Xiao asked the elevator-operator why the new bride upstairs had made such a row, threatening to kill herself in the middle of the night. Taken aback, the elevator-operator replied: 'Did she really? They're having guests over tonight, members of the woman's family. They asked me to give them a hand.' So they were still entertaining as if nothing had happened.

Ah Xiao went out on to the balcony to hang out the washing. She noticed the chair on which the young master had sat when enjoying the breeze of the previous evening. It had been left outside. The weather had suddenly turned cold. A grey sky. Dark, emerald-green trees lined both sides of the street in placid rows like telegraph poles, unmoved by the least flight of fancy. Surrounding the base of each tree was a tight ring of green leaves that looked at first glance like a reflection.

Enjoying the evening breeze now seemed to belong to the distant past. That brown lacquer chair rested unsteadily and creaked as it rocked in the wind as if your average Chinese still sat there on it. On the ground beneath it there were the shells of water chestnuts and peanuts, together with the rinds and pith of persimmons. The tabloid newspaper had been blown by the wind into the guttering, where it remained, sucked firmly against the cement railing by the air. Ah Xiao glanced down and thought to herself with unconcern that there would always be people like that making a mess. Fortunately, however, it was none of her business.

*Translated by Simon Patton*

# TRACES OF LOVE

Although it was just November, they had lit a fire at home, just a small brazier with red-hot charcoal ensconced in snow-white ashes. The coal had been a tree. Then the tree died, yet now, in the glowing fire, its body had come alive again – alive, but soon to turn into ashes. The first time life was green, the second time, a dark red. The brazier smelled of coal. A red date fell into it and started burning, giving out the fragrance of the sweet congee served every year on the eighth of the twelfth month. The coal's minute explosions made a sizzling noise, like grated ice.

They did have a marriage certificate. It was framed and hung on the wall. The upper corners of the picture frame had two rosy-winged cherubs draped with flowing golden sashes; the lower part was a painting in Chinese ink depicting a pool of pale blue water on which two colourful ducks were resting. In the middle was neatly written in clerical script:

Mi Raozheng, native of Wuwei in Anhui Province, age 59,
born 9–11 p.m., 25 February 1885.
Chunyu Dunfeng, native of Wuxi in Jiangsu Province, age 36,
born 3–5 p.m., 9 April 1908.

Dunfeng stood under the picture frame, one knee on the sofa, trying to catch the light as she counted the stitches in her knitting. Mi Raozheng walked over to get his overcoat, saying awkwardly, 'I'm going out for a while.' But Dunfeng kept her head down and kept on counting, her lips moving silently. Mi Raozheng started to put on his coat, walked over to her, and smiled somewhat helplessly. After a while, Dunfeng looked up and said, 'Huh?' She looked down at her knitting again; it was grey, and stippled with tiny knobs of white fluff that looked as if they were caught in its threads.

'I'll be back in a while,' said Mr Mi. He found it difficult to put this into words. He couldn't have said 'going there'; the 'here' and 'there' was just too much. Perhaps 'going to Little Shadu Road'* then – but that would be saying he had one home here, and another home on Little Shadu Road. He used to refer to his other wife as 'her', until Dunfeng objected, saying, 'But no one speaks like that!' After that, on the rare occasion when he referred to her, he used headless sentences.

He said now, 'Quite ill. I've got to go and have a look.'

'Go on,' said Dunfeng laconically.

Something in her voice made Mr Mi feel that he couldn't just go. He put his hands on the windowsill and looked out, mumbling to himself, 'I wonder if it's going to rain?'

Dunfeng looked slightly impatient. She wound the wool up, stuffed her knitting into the floral bag, and made to go out. But as soon as she opened the door, Mr Mi stopped her, trying to explain, 'I don't mean ... All these years now ... Really quite ill, and no one there to look after things. I can't possibly ...'

* Translator's Note: Now Xikang Road in Shanghai. The road first came into being in 1899. Locals still refer to it as Xiaoshadu Road.

This irritated Dunfeng. She said, 'Is there any need to say all this? What'd people think if they heard you?'

Amah Zhang was doing the washing in the bathroom, with the door half open. Amah Zhang had been with his family for a long time and knew everything. She could have thought that Dunfeng was preventing him from going back to see his sick wife. Scandalous!

Dunfeng stood at the door and called out: 'Zhang!' She then gave her these instructions: 'Neither of us will be home for dinner tonight, there's no need to keep the two vegetarian dishes. Put the beancurd on the balcony to keep it cold, and put some ashes on the brazier to keep the fire in, all right?'

She had a different voice when she talked to the servants – a low-pitched, elderly and ill-tempered voice, but also somewhat saccharine, like a madame's. Her chinless chin was pointing upwards, her round face hanging down with its soft fullness, her eyelids half shut. Her classic aquiline nose was also pointing upwards, showing two small noble nostrils. Dunfeng came from an extremely well-established family – one of the oldest merchant families of Shanghai. She was wedded at sixteen, widowed at twenty-three, and only married Mr Mi after over a decade's widowhood. She had a happy life now, but she never went overboard; after all, she was a woman of experience. She touched her hair: it was lifted high in the front, supported by cotton wool underneath, and combed into a horizontal chignon at the back, as neat and orderly as her mind. She gathered her handbag and her carrier bag, and put on her coat. Wrapped in layers of clothes, her white, fleshy body was like a big, solid rice dumpling wrapped in bamboo leaves. Her cheongsam was elegantly cut, not too tight, but for some reason it looked stuffed, as though the lining was woven with thin wires.

Mr Mi walked over to her, asking, 'Are you going out, too?'

'I'm off to my aunt's. It doesn't look as though you'll be back for dinner, anyway, so why bother with the cooking? The two dishes for dinner have been prepared with you in mind – a hot pot and gelatin fish – they're not to my taste.'

Mr Mi returned to the sitting room and stood in front of a desk. There was a stack of stele rubbings with sandalwood covers; he straightened it somewhat. A pale green jade box containing red seal ink, a crackle-glazed brush-holder, a water jar, a brass spoon – everything was cold to the touch. On a cloudy day this home looked particularly clean and tidy.

While he was still fidgeting with things on the desk, Dunfeng came out again. He could only bend slightly forward at the waist because of the stiff coat he had on, and also because of his paunch which had grown with the years. 'Why, you're still here,' said Dunfeng with minimal interest. He smiled and said nothing. She picked up her handbag and carrier bag, and walked out the door; he followed. She pretended not to notice and crossed the road quickly, yet she worried that he'd be puffing behind her to catch up. Though she was angry with him, she did not want him to look like an old man, so she had waited till some cars were coming before she crossed over, thus creating some delay.

She had walked for quite a distance before she noticed that it was raining. Just a drizzle really, more like a chill in the air than rain. Worried that the fur collar of her coat would get wet, Dunfeng wanted to take off the coat, but her hands were not free.

Mr Mi relieved her of her handbag, carrier bag and floral knitting bag, saying, 'Want to take off your coat?' He then continued, 'Don't catch cold. Let's get a pedicab.'

It was only after he had waved down a two-seater pedicab that Dunfeng said, 'You're not going my way.'

'I'm coming with you,' said Mr Mi.

Dunfeng turned her head around in the fluffy black fur collar to cast him a half-smiling glance. She had been brought up by an old concubine of her father's, and had lived in the midst of the concubines of her husband's family, and so had unwittingly developed a brothel-style kind of charm.

Their pedicab turned smoothly into a road in a residential area. On one side there was a small lot: black gravel and brownish grass, and a dark brown house with faded blue venetian blinds standing quietly in the rain. For some reason it looked distinctly foreign. Mr Mi was reminded of the days when he studied abroad. He looked back at the house. A black dog was sitting on the gravel, small curly ears, wet curly fur, body leaning forward attentively, listening or watching for something. Mr Mi recalled that the old gramophones had a dog as a logo; the gramophone played dance tunes, the body heat and scent of Western women rose up from the round collars of their dresses. He also recalled that among his first-born's toys was a green glass dog, about an inch tall, sitting just like the black dog, with red glass beads for eyes. At the thought of the translucent green glass dog, his teeth smarted. Perhaps he had once pretended to chew on it, teasing his child; perhaps he had tried to prevent the child from putting it in his mouth, and out of concern his own teeth could feel the smart – he no longer remembered. His first child was born overseas. His wife was a classmate, Cantonese. In those days there were few Chinese women students overseas, so shortly after he met her they fell in love and got married. His wife had always been neurotic, and later her temper became even more violent, so much so that all her children rowed with her. Fortunately they were now studying in central China, and things had quietened down considerably. He had seldom been with her these last few years.

Even the old days when they were in love seemed to have been muddled through in a hurry; all he could remember were the fights, there were no happy memories to treasure. And yet it was the youthful pain, the anxious years which had truly touched his heart. Even now, as he recalled them, winter and the ash-like rain entered his eyes. He felt a prickling sensation in his nose.

Mr Mi collected himself. He poked his gold-rimmed spectacles higher with his fingers, and shifted slightly in his shirt. It was cold outside, which made the covered pedicab feel particularly warm and clean. This drizzling weather was like a big brown dog, hairy, wet, sniffling up at you with its black icy nose. Dunfeng got down from the pedicab to buy some sugar-roasted chestnuts. She handed them to him while she looked in her handbag for the money. The paper bag in his hands was piping hot, and the heat blurred his thoughts. He could feel her shoulders through her layers of clothes, through the shoulder pads on his coat, and those on hers. This was his woman now, gentle, superior, and quite a beauty a couple of years ago. This time he had not tumbled into marriage; he had made inquiries and plans to make sure that in his old age he would have a bit of peace and a pretty companion to make up for past unhappiness. Yet . . . He smiled and handed her the small bag of chestnuts. She took out two, shelled and ate them. Her face looked red against the black road surface and the brown trees: a face like a flat surface; even her eyes and eyebrows did not have depth, as if they had been painted on the face. And so she looked made up even when she was not wearing any. Mr Mi smiled at her. With the woman of his past, it was rows and fights. With her, sometimes he had to say 'I'm sorry', sometimes 'thank you'. But that was all: thank you, I'm sorry.

Dunfeng threw away the nutshells, wiped her hands together, and put her gloves back on. She felt at peace sitting next to her man. Someone on the street had lifted his gown and was peeing against the wall – didn't he mind the cold? The pedicab went past the post office. Across from the post office there was a house, an old, grey, Western-style house where a macaw was usually hung out on the balcony squawking miserably. Every time she went past this place she was reminded of the home of that husband of hers. She had meant to point the bird out to Mr Mi, but since they were having a tiff she decided not to. She looked up to see the old, greyish-white bird pacing to and fro on its perch; it did not squawk that day. There were two pots of withered red chrysanthemums on the balcony railings, and an amah was bending over to shut the French windows.

The path from the home of that husband to Mr Mi had been a tortuous one. Dunfeng was a woman who put a lot into relationships, a virtuous woman. Even her heartless tailor took advantage of her by pawning the clothes she had had made, causing her much grief, so one can imagine what her marriage had been like. She put the chestnuts into her carrier bag; the paper bag was made of newspaper. She recalled having seen a sheet of newspaper from the *North-east* a couple of days ago – it had been wrapped around some stuff – and on it there had been an ad for a film called *The Trials of Marriage*. She had thought of herself at once. About her marriage, she had given one version to one person and a different version to another, so much so that now even she herself wasn't very clear as to what had actually happened. She would just smile and sigh: 'Oh – it's such a long story.' Even when it had all been settled, one of her brothers-in-law, who had then become a ruffian, had tried to blackmail her, threatening to tell Mr Mi that her husband had died of syphilis. It was a lie, of course, but was there a young man in that family who had not had 606 injections?* Finally it was her aunt who had acted on her behalf and offered some money to hush up the whole thing. She came from a very big family, but except for this aunt's family, she seldom saw any of her relatives. Her brothers were all the old concubine's children. Mr Mi had not met them at all as his original wife was still living, and it would have been difficult to decide on a proper form of address between them. As for Dunfeng, she did not know how to behave to them: if she were to show off her good fortune, they might want to borrow money from her; if she were to tell them her grievances, they might laugh at her. The relatives who had acted as matchmakers were always telling her how much they had done for her. Mrs Yang, her cousin's wife, was particularly irritating with her idiotic boasting. Mrs Yang was the daughter-in-law of Dunfeng's aunt, and this aunt and her son were about the only people Dunfeng felt she could talk to. In fact if she had not been so terribly bored, she would not have paid such frequent visits to the Yangs.

The Yangs lived in an upper-middle-class town house off a small alley. Mrs Yang was at the mahjong table in the dining room. Winter days were short, and the lights had been turned on at 3 p.m. The mahjong table had a leather surface trimmed with metal borders – it had quite a long history. The Yangs had always been a progressive family. When Mrs Yang's father-in-law was head of the family, his children were sent to new-style schools and made to study English. When Mrs Yang's husband had just returned from abroad, he was a real radical. He forced his wife, who had just given birth, to eat fruit and sleep with the windows open; his mother-in-law was not amused. At his encouragement, Mrs Yang became a lively mistress of the house;

* Translator's Note: A widely advertised anti-syphilis drug.

her sitting room had the feel of a salon. Like a French hostess, she received gifts of flowers and chocolates, which were most flattering to her self-esteem. A good number of men came to tell her how unreasonable their wives were; Mr Mi had been one of them. Since he received little consolation at home, he was fond of spending time with other people's wives – just talking and joking with them was enough to make him happy. Because of this, Mrs Yang had always thought that she had given Mr Mi to Dunfeng.

Under the lamp, Mrs Yang's oblong face shone with delight. Two stripes of rouge spread from her eyes down to her jaws – a face all red and white, and all laughter. Her smiling eyes were squeezed narrow, and some loose hair was hanging over them. Though she was not going out, she had an old imitation caracul coat draped over her shoulders. She shrugged her shoulders, grabbing the lapels at her chest to hold the coat in place, and reached for Dunfeng's hand with her spare hand, saying, all smiles, 'Hey, Coz – and Mr Mi. It's been a long time. How have you been?'

When she greeted Mr Mi she did not look directly at him, as if to avoid suspicion. She held affectionately on to Dunfeng's hand and asked again, in a hushed voice, 'How are you?', all the while examining her from top to toe with irrepressible fondness, as though the woman Dunfeng were entirely her creation. Dunfeng hated her for it.

'Is Cousin home?' she asked.

'When has he ever come home so early?' Mrs Yang sighed. 'You have no idea, Coz. How can one still call this a family?'

Dunfeng smiled and said, 'You're really something. Married all these years, and you're still like newly-weds, fighting all the time.'

It was here at the Yangs' that Dunfeng met Mr Mi for the

first time. On that day too, their host and hostess quarrelled in a fashionably foreign manner, like lovers. Mr Mi looked on and felt jealous, though he had no right to be. Because of that he made conversation to Dunfeng, hoping to make Mrs Yang jealous, and then he took Dunfeng home in his car. That was how it had all started . . . If it was indeed true that such a minor incident had started it all, Dunfeng would not have admitted it anyway – her pride would have been hurt. But to say that Mrs Yang was completely out of the picture was not quite the truth either; Dunfeng believed that her jealousy was never without cause.

She still remembered playing mahjong at the metal-rimmed leather table that night. She couldn't afford to lose, but she had to pretend to be easy about it. Now that money was not a problem, she could show herself to be a little miserly, but as a poor relative then she had had to take care that she was generous. Now she had money, but the Yangs, like most families in these difficult times, were going downhill. Though Mrs Yang still had her mahjong parties, the players were different now, mostly young men of questionable background. Dunfeng was rather disgusted with them. The one in a black suit wasn't even wearing a waistcoat. He was seated behind Mrs Yang and just now had said to her, 'Auntie Yang, I'm going to make a phone call. If I get some soap would you like some?' Mrs Yang did not reply. Her coat had slid off her shoulders, and he stroked her back lightly with a finger. She did not seem to feel the tickle, or anything at all. When he turned round to spit, she took a mahjong tile and drew a line right down his back, saying, 'A line has to be drawn – between men and women, OK?' Everyone laughed. Mrs Yang had always had a quick tongue. But Dunfeng thought that, while such behaviour among gentlemen and ladies would no doubt have been considered bold and witty, in the present company it was just cheap.

In the next room someone was playing a flute. To hide her embarrassment, Dunfeng walked over to the door to take a look, and saw Mrs Yang's daughter Yue sitting at the desk with a score in her hands, softly singing a tune from a Chinese opera, accompanied by someone sitting next to her.

'Is Yue learning Peking opera?' Dunfeng asked Mrs Yang.

'It sounds very melodious,' said Mr Mi.

'The two of us will soon be performing together – in *Selling a Horse*. She'll be the male lead, and I the female,' Mrs Yang replied with delight.

'You're still as active as ever, Mrs Yang,' said Mr Mi.

'Oh, I'm merely there for a laugh, but these kids at the Peking Opera Association are real enthusiasts. There's Wang Shuting's daughter, and two of Gu Baosheng's sons. I would not have let Yue join if there were any riff-raff there.'

Someone at the mahjong table asked, 'Auntie, the names of your children all have the word "Hua" in them, how come the eldest young lady is called Yue?'

Mrs Yang smiled and said, 'That's because she was born on the Moon Festival – Yue is the moon.'

Dunfeng remembered all her relatives' birthdays; the poorer she was, the more eager she had been to observe the social niceties so that people would not say things behind her back. She interjected, 'But I remember Yue's birthday is in April!'

Mrs Yang giggled, pulled her coat up and hid her neck in it. Then she walked up close to Dunfeng, looking at her with hazy eyes, and said in a low voice, confidentially, 'She was born in April all right, but her little person was first made on the Moon Festival.'

Everyone heard that, and they were in a riot: 'Oh Auntie Yang –' 'Auntie –!' Dunfeng was embarrassed; for the sake of her family's reputation she couldn't let Mr Mi listen to any more of this. She said quickly, 'I'll go up to see the old lady,' nodded to Mrs Yang and walked away. Mrs Yang acknowledged in kind, saying, 'You two go first, I'll be coming in a minute.'

Dunfeng walked up the stairs ahead of Mr Mi. She turned round to look him in the eye and gave him a wry smile. She had wanted to say to him, 'And you thought she was something precious!' Mr Mi was smiling in a reserved manner as before. Mrs Yang's children appeared on the staircase landing, called out: 'Auntie,' and went their own way.

Old Mrs Yang was very particular about cleanliness, and the children did not dare to go into her room often. This time they had not followed Dunfeng in either. There was a green metal desk in the room, a matching chair, a matching filing cabinet, a fridge and a phone. Because of the Yangs' progressive tradition, even the old lady was fond of new, foreign things. Yet her room was dark, with all the windows shut, and the air made one feel that it was still an old lady's room. Though she had given up opium-smoking, the opium couch was still there. The old lady was lying on the floral quilted padding, reading the papers. The slits of her padded gown revealed a pair of pinkish-purple woollen pants, tied around her ankles with tapes to make them snug. She sat up to talk to them, pulling at the legs of her pants and apologizing with a smile. 'Just look at me! This year the cold weather has come early. I had thought I'd have a pair of quilted pants made, but trousers now cost as much as a gown, so I just have to make do for the moment.'

'We have a charcoal brazier at our place, but it won't do when it gets really cold,' said Mr Mi.

'He's telling me to have a fur-lined gown made. Actually I have two old ones, men's. I wonder if they could be made over,' said Dunfeng.

'That would be best. These old furs are much better quality than what you get now.'

'I'm afraid they may be too small,' said Dunfeng.

'Men's coats are always big, so you should have quite enough material,' said the old lady.

'The ones I have are very narrow at the waist.'

Old Mrs Yang smiled and said, 'So they're yours? I remember you used to dress up as a man. The way you wore a peaked cap, trailing a thick long plait, made you look like an actor.'

'No, they're not my own clothes,' said Dunfeng. Her white, rounded face showed not a trace of embarrassment, and she was smiling serenely, as if it was only right that she should have had an eventful past.

Her late husband was a slight young man. Old Mrs Yang knew it was his clothes she was talking about; so did Mr Mi, and he was none too happy about it. He stood up, clasped his hands behind his back, and turned to look at the calligraphy on the wall. Seeing a little girl peeping at them at the doorway, he walked over and bent down to play with her. The old lady asked the girl, 'Why don't you say hello? Don't you recognize our guest? Now who is he?' But the girl remained shy.

And how else would she address him but as 'Mr Mi'? Mr Mi thought to himself. But the old lady persisted, and now even Dunfeng joined in, saying, 'Say hello, and you'll get chestnuts to eat.'

Irritated by this, Mr Mi interrupted her: 'Let's have the chestnuts.' Dunfeng took a few out from her carrier bag, and the old lady said, 'That's quite enough, quite enough.'

'Aren't you having any, Mrs Yang?' asked Mr Mi.

Dunfeng replied quickly, 'Auntie doesn't eat snacks as far as I remember.'

Mr Mi still tried to persuade her to take some, which embarrassed old Mrs Yang somewhat. She said, 'Please don't stand on ceremony; I really do not eat them.' There were some chestnut shells on the tea table, and the old lady pulled a newspaper over them.

Dunfeng sighed, saying, 'Now even peanuts and chestnuts are priced individually!'

'And the quality gets worse as the price gets higher. They call them sugar-roasted chestnuts, but I doubt whether they use any sugar in the roasting. That's why this year's chestnuts are not sweet at all.' Dunfeng didn't notice the old lady's inconsistency.

'Have you collected your sugar ration yet?' asked Mr Mi.

'No, I didn't see it in the papers today. In fact that's why we have a newspaper delivered every day – to get information about the sugar and rice rations. If I don't take care of these things, no one else in this family will. Well, I never thought that I'd see such times as this in my old age. Perhaps I should go to a fortune-teller and see what the year has in store for me.'

Dunfeng smiled and said, 'Auntie, I was just going to tell you: the other day the two of us went out together and had our fortunes told on the street.'

'Was the man any good?' asked the old lady.

'We were doing it for fun. He only charged fifty dollars.'

'That's very reasonable. What did he say?' asked the old lady.

'Well, he said . . .' Dunfeng glanced at Mr Mi and then continued: 'He said that the two of us will have all our wishes fulfilled, and that he will live for another twelve years.'

She spoke with delight, as though it was an unexpected bonus. To Mr Mi, however, the twelve years sounded rather eerie; he shivered all over. Old Mrs Yang, being of a similar age, felt the same way. She thought that Dunfeng should have been more careful about what she said, and so she interrupted by asking, 'That Iron-mouth Zhang you used to go to, I've heard he's become extremely popular.'

'You can't possibly go to him now. Even with a prior appointment you won't be able to get near him,' replied Dunfeng, waving her hand to emphasize her point.

'These days I seldom hear you mention fortune-tellers. As the saying goes: The poor go for fortune-telling, the rich make offerings to the gods,' said old Mrs Yang, and she started laughing.

Dunfeng was not pleased by what she said, but she was not paying much attention, for she was watching Mr Mi. Mr Mi had returned to his seat, and had looked at the clock as he walked past the mantelpiece. A rather old-fashioned clock with a rectangular red leather case, a gilded face and very slender hands that susurrated; one couldn't tell the time very clearly. Dunfeng knew that he was worrying about his sick wife again.

Old Mrs Yang turned to Mr Mi and asked, 'Are there fortune-tellers abroad?'

'Yes,' replied Mr Mi. 'Some use dates of birth, some use crystal balls, and some use playing cards.'

Dunfeng waved her hand dismissively again and said, 'I've been to foreign fortune-tellers. They're no good! Went to a very famous one, a woman. It was back when my late one was quarrelling with me every single day. *That* she could tell; she said I didn't get along with my husband. I asked her, "What am I to do about it?" She said to me, "Bring him here, and I'll talk to him." What a joke! I don't know how many people at home had talked to him, and it didn't make the slightest difference, so what good would she have done? I said to her, "I'm afraid I can't do it. He won't do what I say because he doesn't like me."

And then she said, "You can bring one of his friends here." Now isn't that ridiculous! What would be the use of bringing his friend? She just wanted more business! And so I never went back.'

Dunfeng went on and on about her late husband. Old Mrs Yang could see that Mr Mi felt extremely uneasy about it: he sat there with his legs crossed, his hands clasped over his belly, his lips pursed in an awkward smile. Mrs Yang interrupted Dunfeng again, saying, 'You mentioned that you wanted a new cook. Our cook Old Wang meant to recommend someone to you. But now he himself has left; he's dealing in merchandise now.'

'It's hard to find help these days,' said Mr Mi.

'Auntie, I don't think you have enough hands now, do you?' asked Dunfeng.

The old lady looked towards the doorway to make sure that no one was there, and then said in a low voice, 'You may not know this, but I'd much rather have a couple less servants around. They'd just be standing behind the mahjong table at the beck and call of your cousin's wife anyway. These days I just ask the alley watchman to do the heavy work, like cutting our firewood; I'd rather give him extra money to do it. Just today your cousin's wife found out somehow that we've been giving him money, and she immediately told him to go out and buy cigarettes for her, as if he were her servant. Now don't you think . . .?'

Dunfeng couldn't help laughing. She asked, 'Does she still provide snacks and meals for her mahjong parties?'

'How can we afford it?' replied old Mrs Yang. 'Everyone has to go home at dinner time, that's why her present group are all people who live in this alley. The only good thing about them is they're easy to get rid of.'

Old Mrs Yang took out a few antique pieces to show to Mr Mi, asking him for an estimate – she was going to sell them. Among these was a big centrepiece painting; the old lady held on to the upper end, and Mr Mi to the lower end, and they stood looking at it. Dunfeng sat herself down on a low stool next to the opium couch, wrapping her fleshy arms around her fleshy knees. She felt that she was a child again, a child protected by the grown-ups, very contented. The world was changing: her auntie had to sell things to make ends meet; her cousin's wife continued flirting and playing mahjong in straitened circumstances – she might have kept up the front of a rich lady, but the truth was saddening. Dunfeng herself was the only lucky one. The risk she had taken with this marriage had paid off. She was now back in the hands of a reliable man, feeling as if she had always been there.

As he looked at the painting, Mr Mi said, 'This is a genuine He Shisun, I'm quite sure of that. But there are a lot of He Shisuns around these days . . .'

The old lady looked at Mr Mi and thought to herself: 'He has a high status in the brokerage, he's well educated in Chinese and Western learning, he's polite, and *so* considerate – and Dunfeng managed to marry him! Dunfeng isn't *that* young, and yet she doesn't seem to have any tact. The way she talks is so hurtful to him, and he just takes it! The times have certainly changed; these days men bow to such behaviour. In the old days she'd never have got away with it. But it's not as if Dunfeng has never suffered at the hands of men, why is she so ungrateful? Mr Mi must be about sixty, exactly my age. Why should I have such a rotten lot and be burdened with a family? – a daughter-in-law who behaves outrageously, and a son so infuriated by her that he doesn't come home much. Everything has fallen on my shoulders. If I could be like Dunfeng, living quietly with my man in a house of our own – just the two of us! I'm an old woman now, all I want is to be free from such cares and worries, nothing else really . . .'

She rolled up the painting, saying, 'I have made an appointment with a dealer tomorrow. Now that you have looked at these things, Mr Mi, I feel at ease.'

Though she spoke casually, her voice conveyed a gentle trust which was very moving. Mr Mi had not received much kindness from women throughout his life, and so he could feel what little kindness there was very keenly. He smiled and said, 'We must invite you to have dinner with us some time, Mrs Yang. I have a few collectibles at home which you might find interesting.'

'I don't dare go out in such cold weather,' said the old lady.

'It's only a short trip by pedicab. When we get a cook, I'll come and fetch you, Auntie.'

The old lady made the appropriate reply while thinking to herself: It's only right that you pay for the pedicab. If I were to go myself, I'd have to have someone keep me company, and you'd have one more person to feed, so it comes out even.

Dunfeng was saying, 'The pedicab is in fact only good for two women sitting together. Two men in a pedicab somehow look rather stupid; and a man and a woman somehow look embarrassing.'

The old lady laughed and said, 'It's certainly awkward for strangers to sit together like that, but with you and Mr Mi, what's there to be embarrassed about?'

'I just can't get used to it,' replied Dunfeng. She thought of herself as a remarkable beauty; as for Mr Mi, except for his glasses, everything about him looked like a baby, small-eyed and small-nosed, as if it couldn't make up its mind whether to cry or not. Under his suit, his back was straight, just like a well-wrapped-up baby – stiff as a board. Dunfeng cast a quick glance at Mr Mi and turned her head. His head and his face were completely smooth – very neat, exactly like a big steamed bun made from No. 3 rationed flour, sitting very solemnly on the collar of his shirt. However knavish her first husband had been, his appearance had never made her feel ashamed of him, ashamed to admit that this was her husband. He died when he was only twenty-five: a long narrow face, well-defined eyes and eyebrows. When he smiled his eyes were wicked!

Mr Mi reached for the papers, and the old lady handed them over to him, asking, for lack of anything to say, 'Have you been to the cinema lately? There's *Six Chapters of a Floating Life*. My granddaughters have seen it and they all say it's very good. There's an old-fashioned wedding, quite interesting.'

Dunfeng shook her head, saying, 'I've seen it. Completely unrealistic. It wasn't anything like that when we got married in the old days.'

'I suppose customs differ,' said the old lady.

'They can't possibly differ *so* much!' said Dunfeng.

The old lady stole a glance at Mr Mi who looked bored. He took up the newspaper, glanced at the page from top to bottom, folded it in half, and as he did so glanced at the clock. Dunfeng said coldly, 'It's getting late. If you want to go, go on.'

Mr Mi smiled and said, 'I'm in no hurry. I'll wait for you.'

Dunfeng was silent. However, he still looked at the clock every so often, and then she glanced at him, and he glanced at her. The old lady was puzzled: there's definitely something to all this. She knew that as a good hostess she should find an excuse to leave the room so that they could say whatever there was to say, but she was too lazy to make the move. Anyway, it serves them right! They're together all day long and have all the opportunity in the world to say whatever they can't say in front of others. Why wait till they're in someone else's home to put on such a show?

Since the topic was the cinema, Mr Mi began to talk about foreign operas, foreign plays, and Balinese dancing. Old Mrs Yang marvelled: 'You've been to so many different places, Mr Mi!'

Mr Mi went on to talk about the temples in Cambodia, where the floors were laid with silver bricks two inches thick, and the statue of Buddha was plated with gold, and the sashes decorated with rubies and sapphires. Dunfeng eyed him with disdain, hating him for worrying about his wife, hating him for not being handsome enough to share a pedicab with her.

'That was the old days. It's impossible to travel any more,' said Mr Mi.

'It'll be easy enough for you to go again when the war is over,' said the old lady.

Mr Mi smiled and said, 'Dunfeng has made it a condition that the next time I travel abroad, I must take her along.'

'She'll be delighted!'

Dunfeng heaved a sigh and said, 'Well, who knows what the future will bring? If both of us live to see the day . . .' She, too, sensed vaguely that this was very hurtful. This was serious, and she was at a loss what to do, so she continued, 'I mean, we don't know who is going to die first . . .' To cover up her blunder she laughed drily.

For a while no one spoke, then Mr Mi stood up, reached for his hat and said smilingly that he was leaving. The old lady asked him to stay a little longer, but Dunfeng said, 'He has to pay a visit somewhere else, so it's better that he goes first.'

After Mr Mi had left, the old lady asked Dunfeng, 'Where is he going?'

Dunfeng sat down on the opium couch, close to the old lady,

and whispered, 'The old woman is ill, he's got to see how she is.'

'Oh? What's she suffering from?' asked the old lady.

'The doctor couldn't decide whether it's bronchitis or not. Just lately he's been going there every day,' replied Dunfeng. Her cheeks looked puffed up with displeasure. Her hands were on her knees – one hand was clenched in a fist, gently hammering one knee; the other was massaging the other knee, up and down, up and down. She was the very picture of sorrow and forbearance.

The old lady smiled and said, 'Why, you should let him go if he wants to. You know very well that he cares about you.'

Dunfeng answered quickly, 'Of course I let him go. First of all, I'm not the jealous type. Besides, I don't have any feelings for him.'

'You're only saying that out of anger,' said the old lady smilingly.

Dunfeng's gaze froze upon the old lady. Her face was all fleshy and powdery, and the only hard thing about it was her eyes. They looked hollow, as if she had rolled them upwards. But she was saying with a smile, 'You know very well how things stand with me. For me, it's just a way of getting a living.'

'But still, you're now husband and wife . . .' said the old lady with a smile.

Dunfeng became agitated. She said, 'I don't hold anything back from you, Auntie. If I had wanted a man, I would not have married Mr Mi.' Her face flushed, she moved even closer to old Mrs Yang and said in a low, laughing voice, 'In fact we seldom do it, maybe once every few months.' Having said this she stared at the other woman, still smiling.

The old lady did not have a suitable reply to this, so she smiled back at her. Dunfeng guessed what the old lady had in mind, and continued before she could say anything, 'I know you're going to say that there's more to a marriage than that, but with someone like Mr Mi, it's difficult to have feelings for him.'

'He really treats you well, and as far as I can see, you don't treat him badly either.'

'Well, even if it's for completely selfish reasons I have to take care of him: what to wear, what to eat . . . I have to make sure that he gets fed properly so he'll live a couple of years more.' Having made such a good joke, she started laughing at it herself.

'Fortunately Mr Mi seems very fit; he doesn't look sixty,' said the old lady.

'Just now when I told you about the fortune-teller on the street – I only told you half of it because he was here. The man said he had a high standing in the business world, and that he would have more than one wife. He also said his wife will die this year.'

'Oh? So she won't be recovering from this illness,' said the old lady.

'Well, I asked the fortune-teller whether I was going to die, and he said it wouldn't be me. He said things would just get better and better for me.'

'I suppose that woman might as well call it quits,' said the old lady.

Dunfeng looked down at her knees as she went on hammering and massaging them. She said with a quiet smile, 'I'd think so.'

An amah came in to say that someone from the boiler room had come to deliver the bath water. The old lady complained, 'I asked for it this morning, and it isn't delivered until now! I have a guest here.'

Dunfeng said immediately, 'Don't think of me as a guest, Auntie. Go and have your bath. I'll just sit here for a while.'

An old labourer carried two buckets of water into the room, splashing water on the floor. The old lady went with him to the bathroom and told him to pour the water into the tub, warning him to be careful not to let his carrying pole dirty her towels.

Dunfeng sat alone in the room, and suddenly everything turned quiet. The neighbour's telephone started ringing. In the silence it seemed to be ringing right in her ear: 'R-i-n-g! R-i-n-g!' over and over again, but no one picked it up. It was like having *so* much to say but no way to say it; the agitation, the entreaty and the urgency were most dramatic. For no obvious reason Dunfeng was shaken by it. She recalled how unsettled Mr Mi had looked in the last couple of days. She did not understand his concern; she did not want to. Dunfeng stood up and, with her arms crossed in front of her chest, stared defensively at the wall. 'R-i-n-g! R-i-n-g!' The phone kept on ringing, and gradually it sounded very sad. It seemed that even this house she was in was empty.

Old Mrs Yang marched the labourer back into the room. Dunfeng turned around and said, 'You can hear the telephone next door very clearly.'

'These houses aren't built properly. The walls are too thin,' said the old lady.

Old Mrs Yang had to pay for the water. There was a stack of banknotes on the mantelpiece, and she gave the man an extra ten dollars as a tip. The labourer wiped the icicles off his whiskers, thanked her and left. The old lady sighed, 'Who'd thank you for a ten-dollar tip these days? This old labourer is a saintly old gent.' Dunfeng laughed along with the old lady.

Old Mrs Yang went into the bathroom. Not long afterwards,

Mrs Yang came upstairs and asked as soon as she walked in: 'Is the old lady having her bath?'

Dunfeng nodded. Mrs Yang said, 'I've hung a scarlet sweater on the bathroom door. I better take it out. The steam in the bathroom will probably fade it.'

She tried to open the bathroom door. Dunfeng said, 'It's probably locked.'

Mrs Yang sat down on the opium couch and pulled her fake caracul coat tighter round her shoulders. Since there was no man around, she had put away all her liveliness.

'How many rounds did you play? How come the game has broken up so early?' asked Dunfeng.

'A couple of them have some business to attend to and had to leave early.'

Dunfeng looked at her and said with a smile, 'You really know how to take it easy. That's a good way to pass the time.'

'Everyone disapproves of me, I know. But the money that changes hands on a mahjong table is negligible – how much can I lose? Now if you look at your cousin, he doesn't come home after work these days, and wherever he spends his time, even if he just sits there, he has to pay! And now everyone says it's my fault, that I've made it impossible for him to come home! This family is now completely dependent on the old lady for everything.' Mrs Yang leaned forward a bit, then continued in a lower voice, 'The situation being what it is, do you think the old lady's mumbling about saving a penny here and there will do us much good? A good few small businessmen living in this alley have made it big. If they were to tip us off in one of their deals, or let us have a small share of it, that'd make all the difference!'

'So you must have made quite a killing,' Dunfeng said.

Mrs Yang leaned back, supporting herself with her arms

stretched to the back, and said sarcastically, 'If we want a share we've got to lay out the money, and money is none of my business here. If I were to take over the management of the household I'm sure she'd pick a big row. But as it is, she complains that I don't do anything.'

All of a sudden she jumped up, pointed to the office desk, chair and filing cabinet, and said with hatred in her voice, 'Just look at this, and this! She monopolizes everything! Look, even the telephone and the fridge . . . I don't care about these things, or else . . .'

Dunfeng realized that the walls were thin. Afraid that the conversation could be overheard in the bathroom, she dared not follow up on the topic, but tried to change the subject, saying, 'The man who was playing the flute downstairs for Yue, who's he?'

'He's also a member of the Opera Association. Yue just keeps to herself too much. Actually her classmates are all on more friendly terms with me, and I try to keep on their good side. When my younger ones have problems with their school work, I just ask them to help out – that saves hiring a tutor. And sometimes they run errands for me. We don't have enough servants here, you know, so that helps. But sometimes they cause me unexpected trouble as well.' She was sitting on the edge of the bed, with her elbows on her knees. Her face was almost buried in her coat and she sniffed at it deeply. Then she said nonchalantly, 'I keep joking with myself – seems that my share of romance is far from over!'

She waited quietly for Dunfeng to question her. When nothing happened she cast a glance at Dunfeng. Some time in the past Dunfeng had been interested in Mrs Yang's encounters, but now her circumstances were different. She was married, and as a married woman she looked at extramarital relationships with a critical eye. No matter how many lovers Mrs Yang had, they could neither marry her nor take care of her financially. Dunfeng put on a solemn expression. To show that only Yue's marriage prospects were worthy of discussion, she asked, 'Does Yue have a friend?'

'I never interfere as far as she's concerned. If I come up with anything, her granny and her father are both sure to object.'

'The man I saw just now, I don't think he's much good,' said Dunfeng.

'You mean the one playing the flute? There's nothing going on there,' replied Mrs Yang.

Yet Dunfeng was a woman with a 'marriage complex'. To her, every man was a possibility until it was proved beyond any doubt that the possibility did not exist. She therefore persisted, 'I don't think he's much good. What do you think?'

Mrs Yang lost her patience. With her chin cupped in her hands, she stamped her foot on the floor and said, 'There's nothing in it!'

'It's true that I only saw him briefly . . . He seems to be the slippery type,' said Dunfeng.

Mrs Yang smiled and said, 'I know the kind of man you like. Looks don't matter that much, but he has to be reliable, gentle and considerate, like Mr Mi.'

Dunfeng was silent, but her face slowly flushed red.

Mrs Yang stretched out her snowy fragrant hand to take hold of Dunfeng's hand. She said with a smile, 'You look so well these days . . . A life like yours can probably be said to be ideal!'

Were Dunfeng to admit to being happy in front of Mrs Yang, she would also be admitting to owing her a favour. That was why she had to complain more bitterly than ever. She said, 'You'd never realize what I have to put up with!'

'What's the matter?' asked Mrs Yang.

Dunfeng bowed her head. Her hands were on her knees –
one hand was clenched in a fist, gently hammering one knee;
the other was massaging the other knee, up and down. Hammering and massaging, she was the very picture of concen-
tration. Her cheeks were puffed out childishly. She said, 'The
old woman's ill. The fortune-teller said that his wife will die
this year. Didn't you see how disgustingly unsettled he looked?'

With half of her face buried in her coat, Mrs Yang observed
Dunfeng with narrowed, judgemental eyes. She thought: 'Now
that she's a concubine she certainly behaves like one! All this
"old woman" stuff. Next she'll be calling Mr Mi "the old man"!'

Mrs Yang laughed and said, 'Wouldn't it be nice if she died?'

Dunfeng was not pleased with her teasing tone of voice. She
replied, 'I don't want her to die. She's no obstacle as far as I'm
concerned!'

'That's true. If I were you I wouldn't care about names and
titles. The important thing is to get your hands on the money,'
said Mrs Yang.

Dunfeng sighed, saying, 'I suppose everyone thinks that I've
made a fortune out of him! Well, of course I know that he'll do
well by me in his will, but if he doesn't bring it up, I can't very
well mention it either . . .'

Mrs Yang opened her eyes wide, working herself up on
Dunfeng's behalf: 'Why, you should ask him!'

'If I do that, won't he have doubts about me?'

For a moment Mrs Yang looked stumped, then she said,
'Don't be foolish! Money does pass through your hands, so you
can accumulate your own nest-egg bit by bit.'

'I don't know how it can be done,' answered Dunfeng. 'Times
are different now. Men are always talking about the price of
rice and coal; everyone knows what things cost. Though Mr Mi
is still with the brokerage in name, he has effectively retired.

His outlay is immense – the upkeep of the children who are all away from home is considerable – it makes sense for us to watch our expenses. And yet at home all the servants have been with him a long time, and they carry on with their old ways. Like last time when Amah Zhang went back to her home village for a visit, there was no end to it! First she said, "Mrs Mi, I would like a few dollars so I could buy some material to give away as presents." Then when she came back she brought chickens, eggs, wholemeal noodles, sticky dumplings . . . We couldn't possibly just accept her gifts. Someday we'll be broke because of this! Every time she wanted something she just thrusts her face in front of me and says "Mrs Mi this, Mrs Mi that". As for Mr Mi, he just encourages them. No matter what it is, he says, "Go and ask the Mrs!" I suppose he means well, letting me do the servants the favours . . .'

Mrs Yang stole a glance at Dunfeng, listening to her repetition of 'Mrs Mi' with a smile. She thought: A veritable concubine!

Old Mrs Yang emerged from the bathroom after her bath and told an old amah to go and scrub the tub. She asked, 'How come there is this smell of steam? Are you ironing?'

Without waiting for the amah's reply she went out to have a look. Sure enough the ironing-board was standing on the staircase landing. The old lady was furious, saying, 'Who told you to do the ironing? Am I the only one to be affected if the fuse blows from overloading? I don't want to be grumbling all day long, but times have changed!'

Amid this bustle Mr Mi arrived. Dunfeng was sitting in the room. Through the open door she could see Mr Mi walking up the stairs, and she was pleased. But she pretended to be surprised, asking, 'Hey, how come you're back?'

Mr Mi smiled and said, 'I was on my way home, so I thought I'd come and pick you up.'

Mrs Yang came out of the bathroom carrying her sweater. Her hands were thrust into the sleeves of the scarlet sweater which she flapped about, hitting Dunfeng a couple of times with them. She laughed and said, 'Just look at how nice Mr Mi is, how considerate! Coming to take you home in this rain.'

Mr Mi brushed his overcoat and said with a smile, 'It's stopped raining now.'

'Do stay for a while longer. You hardly come by these days,' said Mrs Yang.

Mr Mi took off his overcoat and sat down. Mrs Yang glanced at him sideways, smiled, and said very slowly: 'And how are you, Mr Mi?'

Mr Mi replied with a cautious smile, 'I'm fine. And you, Mrs Yang?'

Mrs Yang sighed and answered with a 'Fine'; the sigh went on endlessly.

Dunfeng listened to all this, disgusted with Mrs Yang's pretence, and also angry with Mr Mi for speaking so cautiously, as if afraid that she would make too much out of this. She thought: Frankly, she'll not be interested in an old man like you whatever the case! Do you really think she has her eye on you?

But even now anger gnawed at her whenever Mrs Yang's name was mentioned, partly because there was no new target for her jealousy – she did not feel too strongly about 'the old woman'. Now that she, Mrs Yang and Mr Mi were sitting in a gradually darkening room, she again dug out the skeletal remains of their unformed triangular love affair and relived its memories. She had triumphed. Though it wasn't much of a victory, it counted nonetheless. With faked nonchalance she picked up a cup of tea – a cup of cold tea in the cold house of her relatives. There was a trace of lip rouge on the rim of the cup; she turned it around, only to see another red half-moon stain. She frowned. Her expensive lipsticks certainly did not run, so it must have been that the Yangs didn't wash their cups properly. Who knows who had drunk from it! She turned the cup round again to find a clean spot, but she did not really mean to drink the tea.

Seeing that Mr Mi had come back, the old lady wanted to make sure that Mrs Yang would not have a chance to chat him up, so she quickly sent the amah away and came back into the room. Mrs Yang saw through this and smiled with disgust. She sniffed, and then stood up saying casually, 'I'll tell them to get some snacks.'

She turned to walk away, wearing her coat like a shawl, under which her shapely legs criss-crossed as they made their way delicately out. The old lady was afraid that she would use this opportunity to indulge in buying unnecessary snacks, so she followed her and called out, 'Some baked sweet potatoes will do; they've just come into season.'

'Auntie, there's no need to fuss, we're not hungry,' said Dunfeng. But the old lady ignored her protest.

The old lady and her daughter-in-law stood on the landing instructing the servant to go out for sweet potatoes. Then they started complaining quietly. The old lady said, 'Dunfeng used to be so careful about things like this. She used to be embarrassed about dining at someone's house more than once, and sometimes she would bring some snacks along herself. Now that she doesn't have to be concerned about such things, she thinks that we don't have to count the pennies either . . .'

Mrs Yang laughed and said, 'That's rich people for you. If they don't skimp, they're not the rich.'

Dunfeng sat alone with Mr Mi in the room; for some reason both of them felt slightly embarrassed. Though Dunfeng pulled a long face, she could feel that her eyes were smiling like the new moon.

Mr Mi asked with a smile, 'Well? When do we go home?'

'We wouldn't have anything to eat at home. I told the amah we wouldn't be back for dinner,' Dunfeng replied. Unable to suppress her smile, she asked, 'How come you're back here so quickly? You must have rushed there and back.'

Before Mr Mi could reply, the two Mrs Yangs returned to the room. They chatted as they ate the baked sweet potatoes. There were two left, and old Mrs Yang told the servant to summon the youngest child so that she could have them while they were still warm. The little girl came in, shouting, 'Granny, look! There's a rainbow in the sky.'

Old Mrs Yang opened one of the French windows and everyone walked out on to the balcony. Dunfeng stuck her hands into her sleeves, shivered, and said, 'Now that it's cleared up, it's going to be even colder. I wonder what the temperature is.'

She walked to the mantelpiece to look at the thermometer. It was in the shape of a green glass tower, something she had known well since she was a young girl. The sun was shining on it and a green patch of light was reflected on to the sofa. The sun had indeed come out.

Dunfeng picked up the thermometer. Suddenly the neighbour's telephone started ringing again: 'R-i-n-g! R-i-n-g!' She listened attentively. Someone actually picked up the phone – she was relieved. It was an amah's loud voice, an impatient 'Hello?' which cut off the hesitant pleading at the other end of the line. What followed was a stream of blah-blah-blah; she couldn't tell what was being said. Dunfeng stood there in a trance. When she turned around to look at the balcony, she saw Mr Mi's back. His half-bald head merged into his fat neck.

Behind him, a short, straight section of a rainbow hung in the azure sky – red, yellow, violet and orange. The sun was shining on the balcony. Sunlight on the concrete railings – a heavy golden sheen – momentary, and late in the day.

Mr Mi looked up at the rainbow, thinking of his dying wife. With her death, most of his life would be over, too. The sorrow and anger he had felt when they were living together were forgotten, completely forgotten. Mr Mi looked at the rainbow. His love for the world was no longer love, it became compassion.

Dunfeng put on her overcoat and took Mr Mi's scarf out to the balcony, saying, 'You'd better put it on. It's getting cold.' As she said so, she looked at her aunt and her cousin's wife and smiled apologetically, intimating: It's all for the money, of course. For my own sake I have to take good care of him. We all know what it's about.

Mr Mi wrapped the scarf round his neck and said with a smile, 'We really should go. Thank you for the tea and snacks.'

They said goodbye and walked out to the alley. Under the sheltered walkway someone had set a small stove on a patch of dry pavement. It was smoking and crackling like something alive. In the empty alley one could easily have mistaken it for a dog, or even a child.

They walked out of the alley on to the road. There were few pedestrians and it felt like early morning. Most of the buildings in this area had pale yellow walls, now black and mouldy because of the damp. Parasol trees lined the road, their yellow leaves looking exactly like flowers blossoming in the spring. Against the dark grey walls, the small yellow trees looked particularly brilliant. The leaves at the top waved in the wind and then took off, drawing an arc in the air before overtaking the two of them. Even after the leaves touched ground they drifted a long way off.

In this world, all relationships are frayed and patched up. Still, on their way home Dunfeng and Mr Mi loved each other. Walking on the fallen leaves that so much resembled fallen petals, Dunfeng reminded herself to tell him about the macaw when they walked past the post office.

*Translated by Eva Hung*

# Editor's Afterword

'To be famous,' the twenty-four-year-old Eileen Chang wrote, with disarmingly frank impatience in 1944, 'I must hurry. If it comes too late, it will not bring me so much happiness . . . Hurry, hurry, or it will be too late, too late!' She did not have long to wait. By 1945, less than two years after her fiction debut in a Shanghai magazine, a frenzy of creativity (one novel, six novellas and eight short stories) and commercial success had established Chang as the star chronicler of 1940s Shanghai: of its brashly modern, Westernized landscapes populated by men and women still clinging ambivalently to much older, Chinese habits of thought. 'The people of Shanghai,' she considered, 'have been distilled out of Chinese tradition by the pressures of modern life; they are a deformed mix of old and new. Though the result may not be healthy, there is a curious wisdom to it.'

Chang's own album of childhood memories was a casebook in conflict between the forces of tradition and modernity, from which she would draw extensively in her writing. The grandson of the nineteenth-century statesman Li Hongzhang – a high-ranking servant of China's last dynasty, the Qing – her father was almost a cliché of decadent, late-imperial aristocracy: an opium-smoking, concubine-keeping, violently unpredictable patriarch who, when Eileen was eighteen, beat and imprisoned his daughter for six months after an alleged slight to her step-mother. Her mother, meanwhile, was very much the kind of Westernized 'New Woman' that waves of cultural reform, since the start of the twentieth century, had been steadily bringing into existence: educated and independent enough to leave her husband and two children behind for several years while she travelled Europe – skiing over the Swiss Alps on bound feet. After Chang's parents (unsurprisingly) divorced when she was ten, the young Eileen grew up steeped in the strange, contra-dictory glamour of pre-Communist Shanghai: between the airy brightness of her mother's modern apartment and the languid, opium-smoke-filled rooms of her father's house.

Yet while Chang's fiction was eagerly devoured by the Shang-hai readers for whom she wrote – the first edition of her 1944 collection of short stories sold out within four days – it drew carping criticism from literary contemporaries. For Eileen Chang wrote some way outside the intellectual mainstream of the middle decades of twentieth-century China. Although an early-twenty-first-century Western reader might not immedi-ately notice it from much of her 1940s fiction – the body of work for which she is principally celebrated – she grew up and wrote in a period of intense political upheaval. In 1911, nine years before she was born, the Qing dynasty was toppled by a revolutionary republican government. Within five years, this fledgling democracy collapsed into warlordism, and the 1920s through the 1940s were marked by increasingly violent struggles to control and reform China, culminating in the bloody Sino-Japanese War and civil conflict between the right-wing Nation-alists and the Chinese Communist Party. Many prominent Chinese writers of these decades – Lu Xun, Mao Dun, Ding Ling and others – responded to this political uncertainty by turning radically leftward, hoping to rouse the country out of its state of crisis by bending their creative talents to ideologically prescribed ends.

Despite experiencing firsthand the national cataclysms of the 1940s – the Japanese assault on Hong Kong and occupation of north and east China (including her native Shanghai) – Eileen Chang, by contrast, remained largely apolitical through these years. Although her disengaged stance was in part dictated by Japanese censorship in Shanghai, it was also infused with an innate scepticism of the often overblown revolutionary rhetoric in which many of her fellow writers were taken up. In the fiction of her prolific twenties, war is no more than an incidental backdrop, helping to create exceptional situations and circumstances in which bittersweet affairs of the heart are played out. The bombardment of Hong Kong, in her novella *Love in a Fallen City*, serves only to push a cynical courting couple to finally commit to each other. In the short story 'Sealed Off', two Shanghai strangers – a discontented married man and a lonely single woman – are drawn into conversation in the dreamlike lull that results while the Japanese police perform a random search on the tram in which they are travelling.

Defying critics who scorned her preoccupation with 'love and marriage ... leftovers from the old dynasty and petty bourgeois' and her failure to write in rousing messages of 'youth, passion, fantasy, hope', Chang instead argued for the subtler aesthetics of the commonplace. Writing of 'trivial things between men and women', of the thoughts and feelings of ordinary, imperfect people struggling through the day-to-day dislocations caused by war and modernization, she contended, offered a more acutely realistic portrait of the era's desolate transience than did patriotic demagoguery. 'Though my characters are not heroes,' she observed, 'they are the ones who bear the burden of our age ... Although they are weak – these average people who lack the force of heroes – they sum up this age of ours better than any hero . . . I don't like stark conflicts between good and evil . . . we should perhaps move beyond the notion that literary works should have "main themes".' Eileen Chang was one of the relatively few major Mainland Chinese writers of her period who adhered to the belief that the principal business of the fiction writer lay in sketching out plausibly complex, conflicted individuals – their confusions, frustrations, disappointments and selfishness – rather than in attempting uplifting political advocacy. 'This thing called reality,' she meditated in a deadpan account of the bombing of Hong Kong, 'is unsystematic, like seven or eight phonographs playing at the same time, each its own tune, forming a chaotic whole . . . Neatly formulated visions of creation, whether political or philosophical, are bound to irritate.'

Chang's lack of interest in politics and inevitable antipathy towards the strident aesthetics of socialist realism efficiently guaranteed her exclusion from the Maoist literary canon and impelled her to leave China itself. In 1952, three years after the Communist takeover, as the political pressures on her grew, she decided to abandon her beloved Shanghai, first for Hong Kong and then for the United States, where she lived and continued to write until her death in 1995. In the post-Mao literary thaw, even as Mainland publishers and readers delightedly rediscovered Chang's sophisticated tales of pre-1949 Shanghai and Hong Kong, critics were still unable to rid themselves of long-standing prejudice against her, belittling her work for its neglect of the 'big issues' of twentieth-century China: Nation, Revolution, Progress, and so on.

Begun in the early 1950s, finally published in 1979, 'Lust, Caution' in many ways reads like a long-considered riposte to the needling criticisms by the Mainland Chinese literary establishment that Chang endured throughout her career, to those who dismissed her as a banal boudoir realist. For while the story carries all the signature touches that marked Chang as a major talent in her early twenties – its attentiveness to the sights and sounds of 1940s Shanghai (clothes, interiors, streetscapes); its cattily omniscient narrator; its deluded, ruthless cast of characters – it adds an intriguingly new element to this familiar mix. In it, Chang created for the first time a heroine directly swept up in the radical, patriotic politics of the 1940s, charting her exploitation in the name of nationalism and her impulsive abandonment of the cause for an illusory love. 'Lust, Caution' is one of Chang's most explicit, unsettling articulations of her views on the relationship between tidy political abstraction and irrational emotional reality – on the ultimate ascendancy of the latter over the former. Jiazhi's final, self-destructive change of heart, and Mr Yi's repayment of her gesture, give the story its arresting originality, transforming a polished espionage narrative into a disturbing meditation on psychological fragility, self-deception and amoral sexual possession.

For until its last few pages, 'Lust, Caution' functions happily enough as a tautly plotted, intensely atmospheric spy story. A handful of lines into its opening, Chang has intimated, with all the hard-boiled economy of the thriller writer, the harsh menace of the Yis' world: the glare of the lamp, the shadows around the mahjong table, the flash of diamond rings, the clacking of the tiles. Brief exchanges establish characters and relationships: the grasping Yi Taitai, the carping Ma Taitai, the obsequious black capes, the discreetly sinister Mr Yi. Jiazhi's entanglement with her host is exposed with the slightest motion of a chin, her co-conspirators introduced through a brief, cryptic telephone conversation, the plot's two-year backstory outlined in a few paragraphs. At times, the reader struggles to keep up with the speed of Chang's exposition, as characters and entanglements are mentioned then left swiftly behind: the disappointing Kuang Yumin; the seedy Liang Runsheng; the bland Lai Xiujin, Jiazhi's only other female co-conspirator; the shadowy Chongqing operative Wu.

The suspense reels us steadily along, through the wait in the café, the stage-managed visit to the jewellery store and the ascent to the office, and into the story's startling finale – the section to which Chang is said to have returned most often over almost three decades of rewriting. Chang draws us artfully into her heroine's delusion, enveloping Jiazhi's progression towards her error of judgement in the sweet, stupefying air of the dingy jeweller's office. Afterwards we follow Jiazhi on her sleepwalk out of the store, sharing her surreal confidence that she will be able to escape quietly for a few days to her relative's house, until we wake at the shrill whistle of the blockade and the abrupt braking of the pedicab. Mr Yi's return to the mahjong table brusquely exposes the true scale of Jiazhi's miscalculation: his ruthless, remorseless response, his warped sense of triumph. 'Now that he had enjoyed the love of a beautiful woman, he could die happy – without regret. He could feel her shadow forever near him, comforting him. Even though she had hated him at the end, she had at least felt something. And now he possessed her utterly, primitively – as a hunter does his quarry, a tiger his kill. Alive, her body belonged to him; dead, she was his ghost.'

This final free indirect meditation echoes with Chang's ghostly, sardonic laughter – mocking not only her weak, self-deceived heroine, but also her own gullible attachment to an emotionally unprincipled political animal. For Chang's obsessive reworking of Jiazhi's romantic misjudgement was, at least in part, autobiographically motivated. Like Jiazhi, Eileen Chang was a student in Hong Kong when the city fell to the Japanese in 1942, and she, too, subsequently made her way to occupied Shanghai. Also like Jiazhi, shortly after her return to Shanghai, she entered into a liaison with a member of the Wang Jingwei government – with a philandering literatus by the name of Hu Lancheng, who served as Wang's Chief of Judiciary. In 1945, a year after the two of them entered into a common-law marriage, the Japanese surrender and collapse of the collaborationist regime forced Hu to go into hiding in the nearby city of Hangzhou. Two years later, having supported him financially through his exile, Chang painfully broke off relations with him on discovering his adultery.

Far beyond its specific autobiographical resonances, though, the story's sceptical disavowal of all transcendent values – patriotism, love, trust – more broadly expresses Chang's fascinatingly ambivalent view of human psychology: of the deluded generosity and egotism indigenous to affairs of the heart. In 'Lust, Caution', the loud, public questions – war, revolution, national survival – that Chang had for decades been accused of sidelining are freely given centre stage, then exposed as transient, alienating, and finally subordinate to the quiet, private themes of emotional loyalty, vanity and betrayal.

food

# A Guide to Pronunciation

According to the pinyin system, transliterated Chinese is pronounced as in English, except for the following:

## Vowels

**a**: (as the only letter following a consonant): *a* as in 'after'
**ai**: *I* (or *eye*)
**ao**: *ow* as in 'how'
**e**: *uh*
**ei**: *ay* as in 'say'
**en**: *on* as in 'lemon'
**eng**: *ung* as in 'sung'
**I**: (as the only letter following most consonants): *e* as in 'me'
**I**: (when following c, ch, s, sh, zh, z): *er* as in 'driver'
**ia**: *yah*
**ian**: *yen*
**ie**: *yeah*
**iu**: *yo* as in 'yo-yo'
**o**: *o* as in 'fork'
**ong**: *oong*
**ou**: *o* as in 'no'
**u**: (when following most consonants): *oo* as in 'food'

**u**: (when following j, q, x, y): *ü* as the German 'ü'

**ua**: *wah*

**uai**: *why*

**uan**: *wu-an*

**uang**: *wu-ang*

**ui**: *way*

**uo**: *u-woah*

**yan**: *yen*

**yi**: *ee* as in 'feed'

## Consonants

**c**: *ts* as in 'its'

**g**: *g* as in 'good'

**q**: *ch* as in 'chat'

**x**: *sh* as in 'she'

**z**: *ds* as in 'folds'

**zh**: *j* as in 'job'

# PENGUIN MODERN CLASSICS

**THE WOMAN IN THE DUNES**
KOBO ABE

With a new Introduction by David Mitchell

Translated by E. Dale Saunders

'A haunting Kafkaesque nightmare' *Time*

Niki Jumpei, an insect enthusiast, searches the scorching desert for beetles. As night falls he is forced to seek shelter in an eerie village, half-buried by huge sand dunes. He awakes to the terrifying realization that the villagers have imprisoned him in a steep-sided sand pit with no means of escape. Tricked into slavery and threatened with starvation if he does not work, Jumpei's only choice is to shovel the ever-encroaching sand – or face an agonizing death.

Amongst the greatest Japanese novels of the twentieth century, *The Woman in the Dunes* combines the essence of myth, suspense and the existential novel.

'Abe follows with meticulous precision his hero's constantly shifting physical, emotional and psychological states' *The New York Times*

# PENGUIN MODERN CLASSICS

**WINTER'S TALES**
ISAK DINESEN (KAREN BLIXEN)

'Tales as delicate as Venetian glass' *The New York Times*

After the huge success of her autobiography *Out of Africa*, Isak Dinesen returned to a European setting in these exquisite, rapturous tales of rebirth and redemption.

Beginning with a sailor boy's bold progression into manhood, these stories are full of longing, a theme often mirrored in the desire to escape to sea, as in 'The Young Man with the Carnation' and 'Peter and Rosa'. This collection also includes 'Snow-Acre', a modern rendition of a folk-tale in which old ideals clash with the new order, and is considered by many to be one of her finest stories. Full of psychological insights, these luminous tales reveal the mystery and unexpectedness of human behaviour.

# Penguin Modern Classics

**THIS SIDE OF PARADISE**
F. SCOTT FITZGERALD

With an Introduction and Notes by Patrick O'Donnell

'One of the most wonderful writers of the twentieth century' *Financial Times*

Increasingly disillusioned by the rejection slips that studded the walls of his room and his on/off engagement to Zelda Sayre, Fitzgerald began his third revision of the novel that was to become *This Side of Paradise*. The story of a young man's painful sexual and intellectual awakening that echoes Fitzgerald's own career, it is also a portrait of a lost generation that followed straight on from the First World War, 'grown up to find all Gods dead, all wars fought, all faiths in man shaken' and wanting money and success more than anything else.

*Contemporary ... Provocative ... Outrageous ...
Prophetic ... Groundbreaking ... Funny ... Disturbing ...
Different ... Moving ... Revolutionary ... Inspiring ...
Subversive ... Life-changing ...*

## What makes a modern classic?

At Penguin Classics our mission has always been to make the best
books ever written available to everyone. And that also means
constantly redefining and refreshing exactly what makes a 'classic'.
That's where Modern Classics come in. Since 1961 they have been an
organic, ever-growing and ever-evolving list of books from the last
hundred (or so) years that we believe will continue to be read over and
over again.

They could be books that have inspired political dissent, such as
*Animal Farm*. Some, like *Lolita* or *A Clockwork Orange*, may have
caused shock and outrage. Many have led to great films, from *In Cold
Blood* to *One Flew Over the Cuckoo's Nest*. They have broken down
barriers – whether social, sexual, or, in the case of *Ulysses*, the
boundaries of language itself. And they might – like *Goldfinger* or
*Scoop* – just be pure classic escapism. Whatever the reason, Penguin
Modern Classics continue to inspire, entertain and enlighten millions
of readers everywhere.

'No publisher has had more influence on reading habits than Penguin'
**Independent**

'Penguins provided a crash course in world literature'
**Guardian**

*The best books ever written*

PENGUIN 🐧 CLASSICS

SINCE 1946

Find out more at www.penguinclassics.com